PARANORMAL COZY MYSTERY

Vandals & Yule Scandals

TRIXIE SILVERTALE

Sittin' On A Goldmine
Productions L.L.C.

Sittin' On A Goldmine Productions, L.L.C.

pr@sittinonagoldmine.co

www.sittinonagoldmine.co

ISBN: 978-1-952739-81-1

Cover Design © Sittin' On A Goldmine Productions, L.L.C.

Trixie Silvertale
Vandals and Yule Scandals: Paranormal Cozy Mystery : a novel / by Trixie Silvertale — 1st ed.

[1. Paranormal Cozy Mystery — Fiction. 2. Cozy Mystery — Fiction. 3. Amateur Sleuths — Fiction. 4. Female Sleuth — Fiction. 5. Wit and Humor — Fiction.] 1. Title.

CHAPTER 1

THE SPIRITED ENERGY hovering above me draws me out of dreamland. "Grams, seriously! It's officially winter. Officially the last month of the year. And, officially, Christmas vacation! Can you let me sleep in at least once?"

The ethereal form of my elegant grandmother tugs at a strand of her pearls and smooths her burgundy silk-and-tulle Marchesa gown. Before she can concoct a clever reply, our collective gaze is drawn to the torn hem hovering above her bared left foot.

Only recently, we were involved in a séance that ended as badly as any séance ever has. My grandmother's ghostly existence was kept intact, but she lost one of her priceless Valentinos, and a chunk of her precious dress, to the other side of the veil.

If it hadn't been for the quick actions of my fearless caracal, things could've been much worse. As it stands, the reincarnation of our heroic Robin Pyewacket Goodfellow is becoming more and more like his old self with each passing day.

However, he continues to prefer Sheriff Too-Hot-To-Handle to me.

"Maybe it's a balancing of the power, Mitzy. You know, girls against boys. Erick is spending a great deal of time here, and perhaps it's a good thing that Pyewacket has taken such a liking to him."

Pointing to my lips, I shake my head. She knows better than to thought-drop, but I don't have the stamina to give the speech at this hour. "Whatever you say, Grams. I prefer the old system, where I was Pye's favorite."

Ghost-ma fails to contain a chuckle and presses her perfectly manicured fingertips to her lip. "Of course you were, dear."

"Don't patronize me, Myrtle Isadora! That cat has sacrificed several of his nine lives, saving my hide."

"You don't have to tell me, sweetie. Mr. Cuddlekins is an actual saint in my book. But let's not forget, I'm the savior who won him in an off-the-books Scrabble game and rescued him from a heartless exotic animal dealer. I think I'll always be his true number one."

As you might imagine, Grams' phrase triggers an unavoidable film and television reference. This time my ol' brain bucket locks onto a *Star Trek: Next Generation* line: "Make it so, Number One." I kinda had a bit of a thing for Captain Jean-Luc Picard.

"Mitzy! You're such a hoot."

Folding back the thick, winter-down comforter, I swing my reindeer-onesie-clad legs to the floor, rub the sleep from my eyes, and teeter to my feet. "All right. I'm up. What in all the netherworld was so important that you had to wake me?"

"Have you figured it out?"

I hold up a finger. "Give me a minute, Grams." Stumbling to the bathroom, I splash cold water on my face and rake wet fingers through my Einstein-esque array of snow-white hair. "Figured out what?"

"Mitzy, you're a psychic! You know for a fact that Erick is going to propose. Are you holding out on me? Have you gotten any visions or clairaudient messages?"

"Look. I promised myself a long time ago that I wouldn't use those powers in my relationship with Erick. Sometimes information hits me without warning, but the rest of the time, I stick to the techniques that Silas Willoughby taught me to keep my powers turned down. Now that Sheriff Harper knows all my secrets, it doesn't seem right to use my extrasensory abilities to pry into his subconscious without permission."

Grams spins on her single heel, throws her glowing limbs in the air, and floats toward the ceiling. "You truly are a better woman than I, Mizithra Achelois Moon."

"Tell me something I don't know! I'm sure you remember how easy it was for me to trace my trollop gene straight back to your side of the family tree."

"Well, I never!"

She giggles before I even begin the familiar refrain.

"I think we both know that's not true, Myrtle Isadora Johnson Linder Duncan Willamet Rogers."

The otherworldly tinkle of her laughter follows me as I press the twisted ivy medallion, step through the secret bookcase doorway, and pitter-patter across the thick carpets of the Rare Books Loft.

Down on the main floor, I shiver and make a mental note to add a new heating and cooling unit to the remodeling dream plans. Then I head directly to the back room and add the aroma of sub-par coffee to the thick, musty scent of books—

waiting to be discovered. Once I'm fully awake and dressed, I'll walk over to my grandfather's diner and get a proper breakfast. For now, I simply need to wake up and—

"Grams, where's Pyewacket? I was about to pour him a bowl of his favorite Fruity Puffs, but he's not in his usual spot."

"I haven't seen him this morning, dear. Do you think he's in the printing museum?"

"Could be. Doesn't really matter. We both know he can take care of himself, and when he gets hungry enough—"

"RE-ow." Feed me. The tan terror appears.

Grams gasps and guffaws.

I roll my eyes and open the cupboard. Retrieving the box of sugary children's cereal, I shake it gently. "Is this what you're looking for?"

"Reow." Can confirm.

"Fine, you need to come over here and give me some love, son. You know I'm getting jealous of all the time you're spending with Sheriff Harper."

I swear to you, the furry fiend smiles smugly as he saunters forward.

Before heaping his bowl with a reward, I scratch his broad tawny head between his black-tufted ears.

He nuzzles against my leg and confirms that

even though he's made room in his life for another human, we're still besties.

At some point during the holidays, I'm ninety-eight percent certain that Erick is going to propose. I try to keep my natural snoopiness under control when I'm around him because it obviously means the world to him to surprise me.

However, a girl has her limits. The last time I had lunch with my dad, he was definitely acting ba-jiggity. A sure sign that he was struggling to keep something from me.

The best thing to do is distract myself by dou-bling down on Yuletide cheer. Preparation for the annual Chamber of Commerce-sponsored Northern Lights Yuletide Extravaganza is under-way, and they're always looking for volunteers.

Ever since I was introduced to the concept of mulled cider, or glögg, I've been addicted to the event where it's featured. The mention of addiction makes me look over my shoulder—both literally and metaphorically.

Luckily, Grams must be tucked away upstairs in the apartment. She's not fond of me making light of addiction. Apparently, even though she no longer resides on the earthly plane, she still considers her-self a recovering alcoholic.

Hey, not my job to fully understand. It's simply my responsibility to respect her process.

Tempting fate and hopping over the "No Admittance" chain at the base of the wrought-iron circular staircase, I hustle up the metal treads and get changed.

Once I've had a nourishing breakfast, I'll be ready for anything.

Today's good news: I'm getting more comfortable with the realities of winter weather. Most days, I can survive the half-block walk to the diner, despite the frosty winds whipping across the frozen great lake nestled in the harbor behind my bookshop.

This morning, I have to drive my Jeep. Not because I'm giving up on becoming "winter strong," but because once I finish breakfast, I'll be heading straight to the town square to help wrap light poles in Christmas twinkle lights.

Wow! How fortunate to find a parking spot right in front of Myrtle's Diner. The impending festivities in our sleepy little town have triggered a surge of tourons, and parking is at a premium.

Odell offers me the standard spatula salute as the warm hustle and bustle within the diner embrace me. I claim one of two available red vinyl stools at the counter. The joint is jumping, and Tally's daughter Tatum is sharing the burden with her mother. I toss a quick smile the young woman's way, and she grins and rolls her eyes.

My smile offers an unspoken, "Yeah, I get it. Tourists from down south can be a lot." Meanwhile, Tally places a cup of coffee in front of me and only has time for a quick wink before scurrying off to attend to the rest of her patrons.

My grandpa emerges from the grill in record time and runs a weathered hand through his high-and-tight grey buzz cut. I'd ask him how he knew I was on my way, but I'm starting to suspect that he's more than a little psychic.

"Thanks, Gramps." Inhaling the aromas of freshly scrambled eggs with chorizo and golden brown home fries—all soon to be coated with Tabasco—brings a wide smile to my face.

"That smile should give me the strength to make it through the morning rush." Odell's coffee-dark eyes twinkle as he raps his knuckles twice on the silver-flecked white Formica countertop and hustles back to his kitchen duties.

Since real estate in the diner is in high demand, I power through my breakfast, chug my coffee, and bus my own dishes. But let's be honest, devouring food like a competitive hot dog eater is normal for me on most days. Odell waves. I wink and jump into my Jeep.

Time to make some cheer!

CHAPTER 2

CAR-SIZED FLOES OF ICE jut at angles against the
crisp winter-blue sky. Pin Cherry Harbor's town
square isn't located in the center of town. Rather,
one long edge butts against the majestic body of
water that serves as a major economic port during
the warmer months of the year. The international
harbor will be locked in ice until the spring thaw,
and the Coast Guard cutters break us free.

We're two weeks beyond our most recent snow-
storm, and local snow plow operator and storm afi-
cionado Artie is leading the crew of Yuletide
Extravaganza preparation volunteers.

"Mitzy Moon. Reporting for duty." I pop a
salute, and Artie waves amiably.

"Mitzy, you're with the twinkle-light brigade."
She smirks and points to a group of women with

decades more experience than my measly twenty-four years. Each of the ladies grips a huge plastic tub of tangled twinklers.

I make my way toward the group and offer to pick up the last two tubs. "Where are we taking these tubs, ladies?"

The eldest and self-appointed chairperson, Char, introduces herself and gestures toward a grouping of picnic tables freshly relieved of their burden of snow. "Follow me."

We stack our bins beside the tables and, one by one, test each strand of lights before wrapping them around the branches of the birch, oak, and pine trees bordering the square.

Char volunteers to be my partner and, despite her age, has an agility reminiscent of Pyewacket. With my curves and innate clumsiness, I'm happy to have a cohort comfortable in the branches of these bare-limbed winter trees.

"We make a good team, Ditzy. We're finishing two tubs to every one of theirs."

"That's great. And it's Mitzy."

"Oh! Sorry, Betsy. I must've misheard."

My psychic senses seem to indicate she's sincere, but something about the sparkle in her pale-blue eyes makes me suspect otherwise. Not that it matters. Today is my last day with the volunteers, and then Amaryllis has promised to teach me something called "curling"! And I'm not talking about hair.

Once the complete supply of twinkle lights is exhausted, I offer to make a hot chocolate run to Myrtle's Diner. The twinkle-light brigade cheers in unison.

Odell happily obliges, but the diner doesn't get a ton of large takeout orders, and there's no easy way to transport fifteen hot chocolates. We find a suitable cardboard box in the kitchen, and I place it in the back of the Jeep. It takes multiple trips to carry the steaming cocoas out to my makeshift to-go box.

"Try to drive with a little more caution than usual, kid." Odell chuckles, closes the hatch, and heads back into the diner.

As I return to preparation central, things go pear-shaped—fast.

Two youngsters on cross-country skis whip into the road. You'd think this would be something a psychic would've predicted! However, my special abilities seem to have a mechanism all their own. I have no choice but to slam on the brakes.

The two youths giggle and wave as they pole their way down the street, oblivious to their narrow escape.

The squishy sloshing sound from the rear of my

car turns my stomach. If even one cup of cocoa survived, I'd be shocked.

As I scour the square for my teammates, none can be found.

I track down Artie in the midst of securing one of the food tents to sturdy spikes and offer to be of some assistance. "Thanks, Mitzy. I think the rest of the light brigade headed out early. It's two-for-one at the bingo hall, and those gals are big into bingo—and the early bird happy hour."

"That's all right. I had to slam on the brakes to avoid hitting a couple of kids on skis, so my box of beverages is now more of a slowly draining pool of chocolate. A reject from Wonka's factory."

Her dark eyes dart up as she tugs at her stocking cap. "Those darn kids! I tell them every year not to ski in the streets. If I had a nickel for every time I had a near miss in my snowplow— Well, I'd have a sock full of nickels. That's what I'd have!"

I nod silently. All this talk of nickels reminds me of a book my mother used to read to me before she passed. *A Pickle for Nickel*. It featured a parrot, and the voice my mother used always made me giggle uncontrollably. Over thirteen years since she was taken from me, and I still miss her terribly.

Artie looks over the layout, makes a few adjustments, and smiles proudly. "I have a feeling this year's gonna be the best festival yet, you know?"

Following her gaze, my eyes lock onto the empty space on the lake side of the square. "Where's the ice castle?"

"Oh boy, that's a secret. The folks who put that together are more legendary than St. Nick up here. They only work after dark, and no one's ever managed to catch a photo of the crew in action."

"Oh, wow." Call me a skeptic, but the amount of time it would take to build a life-size castle from blocks of ice—cut right from this very lake—seems substantial. It's highly unlikely that a photographer as talented as the *Pin Cherry Harbor Post's* Quince Knudsen has missed the opportunity to catch the crew in action. If he makes it home for the holidays, I'm going to do a little digging. "Sounds like some kinda mystery."

Artie places a leather-mitten-clad hand on my shoulder. "I recognize that look. Don't you go sleuthing around and ruin the legend."

"Copy that."

"Well, that's about all we're going to get handled today. If you want to come in tomorrow and help me hang out the signs, that'd be swell. If you're too busy, not a problem. I'll get 'er done."

"I'm supposed to start curling lessons tomorrow. Hopefully, the storm that's brewing will hold off for a few more days."

Her sharp eyes widen. "I haven't heard a thing about a storm. What's the scuttlebutt?"

My deadpan expression disappears almost instantly. "I was pulling your leg, Artie. I actually haven't heard anything about a storm. Which is surprising because normally, this time of year, it's the only thing folks are talking about in the diner."

She nods but shakes her head in concern. "It's a bad omen, they say. If there's no snow on Christmas, that's real bad luck."

"Then I'll keep my fingers crossed for a big one."

Artie laughs. "My son Kurt works at the arena. Tell him I sent you, and he'll give you the best sheet." She waves, and I ponder the meaning of "best sheet."

As I return to my cocoa-soaked vehicle, I'm fresh out of ideas. I've never had to clean a vehicle in temperatures below freezing. This might be a job for the world's best boyfriend.

I'm already pressing his number on my speed dial and place the call on speaker, as I collect what trash hasn't frozen in place.

"It's a little early in the day for a corpse, Moon."

"Ha ha. I know you think it's quite hilarious to refer to me as a corpse magnet, Sheriff. But, I'll have you know, I'd be just as happy never finding another dead body."

This comment brings uproarious laughter. "Oh, wow, Moon. Cheers to you for that toss from left field. What's up?"

Now that I have to explain the situation to him, it seems fairly mundane and a bit embarrassing. Attempting to leave out any details that may lead him to believe any part of the situation was my fault, I eventually get around to making my point. "So, I've never had to wash frozen hot chocolate out of a car. I don't even know where to begin."

"And you thought this micro disaster was something that the sheriff's department should handle?"

"Rude. I thought it was something my *boyfriend* could handle." His warm laughter makes my tummy flip flop, but I'm not going to give him the satisfaction of letting on.

"And there it is. Tell you what, I'll give Clarence a call and let him know you're on the way. He has a couple of heated bays at his shop. I'm sure he'd be happy to let you pull in there and scrub away."

"So you're pawning me off on another man?" I wish he could see my fist on my hip.

"Nice try, Moon. You'll be in good hands with Clarence, and I'll make it up to you by bringing a nice hot lasagna from Angelo and Vinci's and a bottle of Chianti to your apartment tonight. Deal?"

Tingles circle my vertebrae, and an unstoppable smile curls the corners of my lips. "I guess."

Erick makes an air kissy sound and ends the call.

To be fair, the local mechanic, Clarence, is a standup guy. His shop is cleaner than my rundown apartment back in Sedona, Arizona. Boy, do I not miss that dive.

When the wizened form of Silas Willoughby showed up outside of my should-be-condemned door and handed me a copy of Myrtle Isadora's last will and testament, a strange key, and a wad of cash, I had no idea it would lead me to this amazing new life. Every once in a while, I miss a sliver of what passed for my old life, but as time marches on, those moments become fewer and farther between. In fact, I'm starting to long for small towns, community festivals, and routines. The touchstone of eating several meals a week at a restaurant named after my not-so-dearly-departed grandmother has given me a sense of comfort I never dreamed possible.

CLARENCE HAS WHAT HE CALLS "an ear for engines." He must've heard my Jeep rounding the corner. As I pull into his parking lot, one of the bay doors lifts, and he waves me in.

Rolling down my window, I offer a folksy greeting. "Afternoon, neighbor." Technically, we're all neighbors in Pin Cherry.

"Good afternoon, miss. A certain Sheriff Harper says you've got a cocoa crime scene on your hands."

The phrase cocoa crime scene hits me square on the funny bone. I laugh so hard tears leak from the corners of my eyes, and I can't get myself lined up with the garage door properly.

Clarence knocks on the hood to put a halt to my shenanigans and offers to finish the task.

Once he's pulled me in between the uprights of the lift, he sets me up with his wet-dry shop vac, a bucket of sudsy water, and a fresh-brewed cup of instant hot chocolate.

Where did this guy learn to be so thoughtful? "Are you married?"

Now it's his turn to laugh uproariously.

CHAPTER 3

THE REST OF MY TIME with the single-and-not-looking-to-mingle Clarence passes without incident. My vehicle is definitely clean-adjacent, and I make it home in time to freshen up before my lasagna—I mean, my boyfriend—arrives.

BING. BONG. BING.

"He's here!" As usual, Ghost-ma's voice joins mine in the cry.

"Yes, *he* is. Time for you to spirit away to the printing museum, dearest grandmother."

"Don't I even get to say hello?"

"Since Erick can neither see nor hear you, why don't I just pass along your greeting? Which is pretty much what I would have to do anyway."

She rolls her eyes and disappears with a huff. A

voice from the ether calls back to me, "You should tell him about the vision you had. I think he would be very interested in discussing remodeling our printing museum into a gorgeous apartment for the two of you!"

"Grams! Stop pressuring me. Besides, you know Erick lives with his mother and takes care of her. Her eyesight is seriously failing. Macular degeneration is no joke. There are real-world problems at play here. Now, go busy yourself planning a wedding that may or may not happen!"

When the bookcase door slides open, the fuming face of a furious ghost pops into the visible spectrum mere millimeters from my nose. "Do not even joke about the wedding not happening. I'm happy to let the man propose in his own time, but that time best be soon."

She vanishes before I can point out the blatant contradiction in her statement. Never mind.

When I reach the back door, I take a moment to compose myself before closing my eyes, puckering my lips, and pushing the door open.

"Do you want me to kiss you, honey? Or did you think it might be someone else?"

My eyelids flip open like a broken jack-in-the-box lid, and I take in the sight of my petite stepmother.

"Amaryllis? I thought you were—"

She snickers and tosses her auburn curls over her shoulder. "Let me guess. Erick?"

My cheeks turn an unflattering shade of red. "Um, yeah. What's up?"

She places her hand on her cheek and shakes her head in dismay. "I wanted to let you know we'll have to cancel your curling lesson."

I'm not the best actress in the world, but I attempt to feign disappointment. Gesturing to my father's Restorative Justice Foundation across the alleyway, topped by the penthouse where he, my stepmother, and my adopted stepbrother when he is home from college, reside, I ask, "Is everything all right with you and dad? Do you need me to help with anything?"

She glances over her shoulder and pushes away my concerns with a flick of her wrist. "Oh, it's nothing to do with us. I got a call from the team captain saying the curling club is on fire!"

I'm about to ask additional questions when the antique mood ring on my left hand encircles my finger in a band of icy chills. Glancing down, I see flames leaping several feet into the air and black smoke billowing into the darkening night sky. At first, it seems like a simple confirmation, but then a voice from beyond cries out. "Help me! Someone, help me!"

My eyes widen to saucers, and I grip my stepmother by the shoulders. "Someone is trapped in the building. We have to get over there."

Amaryllis grabs my hand and runs toward the middle of my three garages. She types in the code. We jump into the Jeep, and I grab the keys from the sun visor. As I fishtail onto the street, a sudden thought occurs. "Where am I going? I have no idea where the curling arena is."

"Head toward the marina. It shares a home with the hockey ice rinks."

"Copy that."

She nods and gives verbal directions while I navigate the snowy streets.

As soon as I make the turn toward the marina, the orange glow filling the night sky sends a stabbing pain to my gut. I hope we're not too late.

We haphazardly ditch the vehicle in the middle of the parking lot and run toward the flashing lights of the fire trucks. Amaryllis may be small in stature, but her reputation as a brilliant attorney and a woman who gets things done precedes her in this town.

She shouts through the chaos, "Where's the fire chief?"

A woman dragging an additional hose off the truck points to a group of firefighters positioned between the trucks.

Amaryllis nods, and I follow her toward the

chief. "Chief, we have a report that there's someone trapped inside."

He turns, takes a moment for visual identification, and nods. "We heard the same, but no details. Is yours a reliable source?"

She confirms with a nod.

He grumbles with frustration. "Can you be more specific? You know how big this place is. I don't want to lose one of my best firefighters chasing smoke and shadows in there."

It seems she and I have the same thought at the same time. She turns toward me, and we simultaneously shrug our shoulders.

I can't exactly explain that my information is based on extrasensory perception. Think. Think. Think.

"Amaryllis, can you give me details?" The chief presses her for more.

Grabbing my phone, I pretend to be getting additional information while desperately calming my heart rate and reaching out to the trapped individual with every tingling fiber of my psychic abilities.

"She's on the phone with the tipster, chief. Give her a second."

Never let it be said that Amaryllis isn't quick on her feet. Of course, it stands to reason that my father would choose someone he'd describe as intelligent first and beautiful second.

Pushing distractions from my mind, I hone in on the desperate plea. "The storeroom beside the Zamboni."

Amaryllis turns to the chief. "The person is trapped in the supply room next to the Zamboni. You know the one. It's at the far end of the hockey rink. Built into the wall that separates the rink from the curling club."

"10-4."

The chief steps away, shares his intel with a firefighter, and we all hold our collective breath as the brave soul adjusts his helmet and runs into the burning building.

Sirens wail in the distance, and my heart flutters with the knowledge that Erick is seconds away. Meanwhile, the onshore breeze is blowing the acrid smoke in our direction, and my bare hand isn't much of an air filter.

The tall, broad-shouldered shape of my handsome boyfriend jogs from the shadows of the parking lot into the glow of the inferno. He clocks my presence a stride before recognizing Amaryllis. "I can't believe I'm saying this, but I'm actually not surprised to see the two of you here. What's the situation?" He hands us each a handkerchief that we eagerly accept.

"Someone is trapped inside," I speak through the cloth filter and take a shallow breath.

He shakes his head and strides toward the fire chief for something called a situational update.

Amaryllis grips my hand and squeezes hard. "I hope we got here in time. Any idea who's trapped?"

"I didn't get a name. I only heard the cry for help. Honestly, I didn't even see a face."

"It's okay, Mitzy. You did everything—"

"Holy *Backdraft*, Batman!" My jaw drops like a motocross starting gate, the handkerchief flutters toward the muddy snow, and I point in awe.

The hulking silhouette of the firefighter, with a body slung over his shoulder, darkens the burning doorway. Flames lick the sky, and smoke swirls ominously around the figure.

The chief runs forward and helps transfer the victim to a waiting gurney. As paramedics take over, Erick steps into the fray to get an identification.

He says something to the chief and returns to us. "It's Kurt Frazier."

I shrug and shake my head. "Should that mean something?"

"Kurt grooms all the ice here—from the rink to the curling sheets. He's Artie's son."

My stomach heaves uncomfortably, and I'm wondering if my instant hot chocolate is about to make an encore appearance.

Amaryllis slips an arm around my shoulders as I shake uncontrollably. It's only now that I realize I left without a coat. The adrenaline and the preoccupation must've kept the cold at bay.

Erick slips off his uniform jacket and places it around our shoulders.

Tears well in my eyes as Amaryllis rubs my shoulder and whispers softly. "It's going to be okay, Mitzy. We have to believe it's going to be okay."

A labored coughing as the paramedics lift the rolling gurney into the back of their vehicle sends a surge of hope to my heart.

Sheriff Harper exchanges words, and the ambulance heads toward the hospital.

"They said it's looking good. Definite smoke inhalation, but his pulse is strong, and he appears lucid."

Amaryllis hugs me tightly. "You saved another one, Mitzy."

Tears roll down my cheeks. Before I have a chance for a proper celebration, a clairaudient message drifts from the netherworld to my consciousness. *Arson.*

Gripping Erick's shirtsleeve, I pull him close and whisper the news.

"You're sure?"

"As sure as I can be. Are you gonna tell the chief?"

"The hockey arena is one of the oldest buildings in town. It had a recent facelift, and one could assume it passed all of its inspections. However, hockey is almost a religion in these parts, so it's possible that some corners were cut. Most likely the fire started from some old frayed wires . . . I can talk to the chief and see if he'll agree to a more thorough investigation—based on my hunch. Buuuuut, at this point, with no proof, I can't really push my agenda."

"Understood. If I get anything else, I'll let you know." A full-body shiver grips me, and my teeth chatter audibly.

He leans in, kisses my cheek, and whispers, "You and Amaryllis can head home. I'll have some paperwork on this, but I can still bring dinner if that's okay?"

My shaky hand reaches for his. "I would really like that."

He smiles, slips his jacket off our shoulders, and winks. "Then consider it done, Moon."

CHAPTER 4

AMARYLLIS OFFERS to drive us home. I accept her generosity without complaint. Something about the fire shook me. Maybe it's memories of the old building burning down next to the bookshop. My father has rebuilt his headquarters since that fateful day, but I'll never forget the panic that seized my chest when I thought Jacob Duncan might've been trapped inside. Better distract myself with some chatting.

"I'm glad they got Kurt out of that mess. Do you think they got to him in time?"

"You know Artie, right?" Amaryllis smiles confidently.

"Yeah. She's a pistol." My weak grin is no match for hers.

"Exactly. Kurt comes from strong stock. His father is an ice-road trucker! If that gives you any idea what his DNA might be capable of enduring." Amaryllis taps her thumb on the steering wheel and smiles.

"Thanks. I just don't want to lose anyone this time of year, ya know?"

Amaryllis sighs. "Oh, I hear you. Let's not forget, my anniversary is coming up in two short weeks. No black clouds on my special day, okay?"

"Oh, my gosh! It's not that I forgot . . . the fire is just distracting me. Are you and dad taking a second honeymoon or anything?"

"Not exactly." The low rumble of her chuckle intrigues.

"What does that mean?"

"Stellen gets home tomorrow, and it sounds like he and Yolo Olsen are 'on again.'"

My stepbrother and his brilliant elfin girlfriend always bring a smile to my face and a spark of hope for true love to my heart. They're both driven by their intellectual passions, and their relationship fades in and out of fashion. "Well, that's great. What does that have to do with you and dad taking a second honeymoon?"

"One thing your father definitely inherited from Isadora, post-alcoholic Isadora, that is, is family first. We had planned a little Caribbean island getaway, but once he got word of Stellen's plans, he postponed the trip. Instead, we'll all be having a stay-cation. He promises plenty of movies, board games, takeout, and endless snacks."

Laughter finally eases the tension in my shoulders. "Throw in some volunteer hours at Doc Ledo's vet clinic, and that sounds like Stellen's dream vacation!"

We share a chuckle as she turns down the alleyway between our two buildings and pulls into my garage.

Walking through the lightly falling snow together, she sticks out her tongue to catch a flake or two. "Hopefully, this is a good sign. Everyone loves snow at Christmastime."

Artie's earlier prediction echoes in my mind. "Yeah, I heard it's a bad omen if there's no snow at Christmas."

Amaryllis grips my goosebump-covered arm. "That's right! A lot of predictions are based on snow this far north. Speaking of which, you better get inside before you catch your death, young lady." She pauses while I unlock the side door, then squeezes my shoulder and adds, "Let me know if you need anything. Okay?"

"I will. We've got to think happy thoughts for Kurt. Plus, I'll get Grams and set up an arson wall. Hopefully, I won't have to edit that to include murder."

Amaryllis points to the night sky. "From your mouth to God's ears, Mitzy." She jogs across the alley to her door as I duck inside the Bell, Book & Candle.

Grams blasts through the wall from the printing museum. "Did I hear you say *murder*?"

"Yes, but it hasn't happened yet."

"Did you have a premonition, dear? If your powers have grown to the point where you're able to predict a murder before it happens—"

I wave my hands like an airport marshaller on the tarmac. "No. No. Simmer down. It's nothing like that." Then I fill her in on the events at the arena and Kurt's prognosis.

"He's one of the nicest boys in all of Pin Cherry. How he managed to stay single, I will never know!"

My eyes roll of their own accord. "I know you might find it hard to believe, Grams, but some people choose to be single."

She offers a haughty scoff in my direction. "Maybe that's what they tell themselves."

"Oh brother."

Before we can continue our debate, Pyewacket leaps from the top of a bookcase and nearly causes me to have a pants accident.

"Pye! I've only recently gotten Grams under control. I don't need ghosts or demon cats scaring the daylights out of me! No leaping from high places! Please." I hastily add the polite plea in case it makes some kind of difference.

Uncharacteristically, Pyewacket makes no response. Instead, he pushes up on his hind legs, and something clenched between his fangs catches the light.

"Well, well, well. It seems our furry overlord has a clue." I gently remove the item from his mouth and examine it. "Grams, is this Grampa Cal?"

She looks over, or rather through, my shoulder and smiles. "Oh, he was so handsome! Although, I was never a fan of that sport."

"And which sport is that?" I stare at the photo in utter confusion.

"He was captain of the curling team."

"Seriously? This—whatever he's holding—is curling?"

"Oh, yes. If I remember correctly, he made the winning shot, or slide, or whatever they call it, with that stone."

An intense negative energy hangs in the air. "What is it you don't like about curling?" I wipe the feline slobber from the corner of the photo and await a response.

She refuses to make eye contact and fiddles with one of her many strands of pearls.

Whether it's a psychic message or good old-fashioned women's intuition, the answer comes to me too easily. "Oh, I get it. Nights out with the boys at the curling club cut into *Isadora* time. Am I getting warm?"

She exhales loudly, and her designer-gown-clad shoulders slump. "I worked so hard to get sober, sweetie. I only wanted the family to spend as much time together as possible."

"Partners having interests outside of the relationship can be healthy, Grams."

"Perhaps. However, with your Grandpa Cal, those interests tended to wear skirts."

My mouth forms a silent "O." "I see your point. Did he ever act on those impulses, or was he merely a hopeless flirt?"

"In my heart of hearts, I believe he was merely a hopeless flirt. However, he did take up with that ridiculous Lillian Barnes rather quickly after we separated."

Something about her tone sends me a clear "off limits" message. I turn my attention to Pyewacket. "Thanks for the picture, Pye. Usually, you're ahead of the game. I'm sorry to inform you, your Royal Pye-ness, but I'm already aware of the fire at the curling club."

Pyewacket instantly turns his back to me and struts away as though he finds humans beneath him.

"Ahem, I'll remember that attitude the next

time you're scratching at the cupboard door waiting for your favorite treat."

"RE-OW!" Game on! And with that, he rockets up the circular staircase and vanishes onto the mezzanine.

Grams whooshes after Pyewacket, and the human stands alone.

By the time I arrive in my swanky, secret apartment, Ghost-ma has the rolling corkboard front and center, and she's already made out a 3 x 5 card for Kurt Frazier.

"It's not a murder wall this time, Grams. We're trying to solve an arson. I don't know if we really need a card for Kurt. It seems like the person who did this had something very specific against hockey or curling, not necessarily Kurt himself."

"You're the one who always tells me not to jump to conclusions, dear. And Kurt isn't out of the woods yet. I know we're all praying for the best, but if he doesn't make it for some reason, then your arson becomes a murder."

Another shiver passes over me. "Let's definitely not put our eggs in that basket. Amaryllis said that the Fraziers come from strong stock. Did you know Kurt's dad is one of those crazy ice-road truckers?"

Grams giggles. "I have to say that's the nicest way I've heard that put."

"What are you getting at?" I tilt my head and lift my chin.

"Artie and Marc unofficially parted ways well over a decade ago. The only reason people try to put a positive spin on the story is because Marc always sent her money for Kurt and his brother. However, the means by which her absentee husband acquired the money is somewhat less than innocent. Last I heard, he was running drugs for a foreign cartel working out of a base in Canada. So whether he's driving them on icy roads or not is hardly the point."

"Oh. You sound legit judge-y, Grams. Are you sure you have your story straight?"

Her shimmering hand balls into a fist, and that fist immediately goes to her curvy hip. "I never jump to conclusions where illegal substances are concerned. And you should know better than most that I do not joke about addictions. Dealing and doing drugs is no way to make money, even if those funds are going to support a wife and children. Marc Frazier was always onto some new get-rich-quick scheme. So if we're basing this investigation on what type of stock the Fraziers come from, I think it's fair to include the fact that there could be a bit of the father in the son."

My stomach gurgles uncomfortably. "Do you

think Kurt was doing something illegal? Maybe using the curling club as his base of operations?"

Grams waves her hands in surrender. "Don't take my words out of context. It's quite possible that Kurt is more like his mother than his father. I'm simply putting forth the hypothesis that this case may be more connected to Kurt than you assume."

"Fine. The card for Kurt stands. I think you better make one for Marc Frazier while you're at it. If he's still involved in illegal trafficking, we have to be open to the possibility that he got his son involved."

Grams tugs at the edges of her Marchesa gown and curtsies. The torn hem flutters, and she moans. "I'll probably never see that beautiful silver Valentino slingback again. Shame. Terrible, terrible shame."

Walking toward her, I attempt to grip her ethereal hand. "The true shame would have been if we lost you, Grams. Thanks to Pyewacket's quick thinking, all you lost was a shoe and a bit of a dress."

She presses her hand to her ample bosom. "A bit of a *dress*? You've never truly appreciated couture, Mizithra."

I offer her a halfhearted smirk. "I guess not. Call me crazy, but I tend to appreciate people more than things."

She looks away.

If ghosts could blush.

"Let's get back to the investigation, Grams."

She nods and returns to the stack of 3 x 5 cards. "Anyone else?"

"Absolutely no one. If Kurt is feeling better to-morrow, I'll head over to the hospital and see what he can tell me. If he's involved, I'm sure my psychic antennae will pick something up during our con-versation."

Grams points an eager finger in my direction. "That's a wonderful idea. You and your abilities will have him on the ropes in no time."

"Whatever you say."

At long last, the doorbell rings, and I allow Ghost-ma to accompany me to greet Erick.

"Good evening, Sheriff Harper. My beloved grandmother would like to offer you a welcome to our humble bookshop."

Erick snickers, runs a hand through his slicked-back blond bangs, and steps inside. "Good evening, Isadora."

She moves toward him, and he shivers.

Observing the reaction is still a novelty to me. Since I've always been able to see and hear Grams, I've never gotten ghost shivers when she comes near me—or passes through me!

Rubbing his shoulder, I attempt to bring him back to my earthly dimension. "I'll grab some forks and napkins. Is it all right if we eat up in the apartment?"

He nods. "That sounds great. I'd really like to kick my boots off and—"

Grams whirls like a dervish. "Oh, dear! That sounds like my cue to exit, stage left."

Her hilarious imitation of Snagglepuss, the cartoon mountain lion, sends me into a fit of giggles.

Erick knits his brow. "I feel like I missed something."

"It's not worth repeating. Just Grams up to her old tricks. Anyway, she'll be giving us some privacy. I'll meet you up there, Sheriff."

"10-4, Moon."

I happily watch him walk away before darting into the back room to grab supplies. To be fair, I'm not sure if it's Erick or the aroma of scrumptious lasagna that draws me upstairs faster.

CHAPTER 5

WHEN THAT FIRST bite of cheesy, saucy, pasta goodness hits my palate, I nearly swoon. "This has to be the best lasagna I've ever eaten."

Erick makes a non-verbal sound that mimics agreement, but he shrugs and tips his head from shoulder to shoulder. "It's good. But you haven't tasted the world's best lasagna until you've had mine."

"You cook? Like, not heat things up in a microwave, but actually cook?"

He wipes tomato sauce from the corner of his mouth and grins mischievously. "There are so many things you don't know about me, Mitzy Moon."

"If I were you, I wouldn't act so smug about it, Sheriff. I'd know a lot more if I didn't respect your boundaries."

The look of confusion on his face is quickly replaced with concerned understanding. "I always wondered if you used your powers on me. I didn't have the nerve to ask."

After a swallow of Chianti for courage, I attempt a version of the truth. "Before we were, um—an item, I may have crossed the line a couple times. But ever since things became more serious between us, I made a vow not to pry. Sometimes things come at me out of the blue, and I try to close off my receptors as quickly as possible. But I never go digging. I wouldn't do that to you."

His broad smile warms every part of my insides. "I appreciate that about you, Moon."

The little orphan trapped inside of me longs to beg for more compliments. The grown-up heiress/philanthropist takes a different tack. "When will I get to taste this legendary lasagna?"

He glances around my apartment and shrugs. "Well, if you had a kitchen in here instead of a museum for fashion, I would be happy to make a pan of it right now." Erick shakes his head playfully. "Thing is, it requires more than a coffee maker and a microwave."

His reference to my sparsely furnished back room downstairs does not carry the insult he intends. "I'll have you know, that closet, which I happily refer to as *Sex and the City* meets *Confes-*

sions of a Shopaholic, was Isadora's prized possession."

We share a chuckle, and after another sip of wine, I broach the subject I've barely been able to keep at bay. "I don't want this to come off wrong, and I'm definitely not pressuring anyone, but—"

He holds his wine glass between us as though it possesses protective powers. "If this is going where I think it's going, please don't pressure me for details."

My intention had been to discuss future living arrangements, but the look on his face and the words "pressure me for details" trigger an image of a snow princess. "Erick Harper, you better not have nominated me for another one of Pin Cherry's ridiculous seasonal royalty contests!"

He covers his mouth with a napkin and laughs uproariously. "Just say whatever you want, Moon. No secrets between us. Okay?"

"All right, I guess. I want you to know this was only a dream or possibly a vision, and I'm in no way trying to force my ideas on anyone. But I keep thinking about what kind of living arrangements we would have, if— You know."

He nods solemnly and runs his left thumb along his stubbled jawline. "If I didn't know any better, I'd say it's funny that you bring it up. Since I happen to know the secret about your special abilities, I find it charming that we're on the same page. Yesterday my mother told me she's finally had enough of winter. After Christmas, she plans to move to Florida with her younger sister, permanently. She cried a little, but I told her I would fly her up to visit any time she wants."

My heart skips a beat as I realize what this means. One of the barriers to Erick and I being together, as in every day together, has been removed. "Absolutely! I will gladly chip in, too. I love your mom. Gracie Harper is a force to be reckoned with. I'll never forget the way she took over the sheriff's station when they put you in that holding cell."

He rubs a hand across his face and shakes his head. "Yeah, she's definitely the reason I turned out as well as I did."

I scoot closer to him and whisper in his ear. "And you turned out amazing."

As usual, he calls my bluff, and, in the blink of an eye, my wineglass is on the coffee table, and his soft pouty lips are on mine. I'm no fool. I enjoy the dazzling kiss before I continue my discussion of living arrangements.

Coming up for air and fanning the flush from my cheeks, I dive back in. "So let me tell you what I was thinking. You know how important Grams is to me, and she can't exactly move to Florida. However, she is willing to donate everything in our printing museum collection to some international printing museum in California. That would leave us three stories to renovate as we see fit. I had some ideas on that. Do you want to hear them?"

Erick scoops his arm around me and nuzzles my neck. He's clearly more interested in renovating my person than hearing about my remodeling plans for the adjacent museum. "Sure. Dazzle me."

Here goes nothing. "Starting on the ground floor, I was picturing a large open-plan kitchen with an enormous living room and a formal dining room. Maybe a cozy fireplace in the living room?"

He nods enthusiastically. "Seems like a good idea. You're always cold."

Snuggling closer, I murmur, "Not always."

Erick kisses the top of my head. "You better continue—while you still can."

"All right. Simmer down, Harper. On the second floor, there would be two gorgeous gue-strooms, each with en suite and sizable closets. And also a small seating area next to a second fireplace that could make a cozy reading nook."

He nods.

"Continuing up the stairs to the third floor, there could be another lovely seating area, complete with floor-to-ceiling bookcases and comfy over-stuffed furniture. Then a small built-in desk in the corner, but work wouldn't be the focus of this area."

"Oh, really? What would be the focus?" He kisses my neck.

"Don't interrupt. I'm getting to the best part." My attempt to be stern only eggs him on.

"You have my attention."

"The primary suite would be on the top floor. Spacious and beautiful—and with its own fireplace."

Erick chuckles. "Of course."

Outwardly, I roll my eyes, but inside I feel like this place already exists. "There'd be a lovely walk-in closet, not quite as big as the one in here, but still larger than my crappy old apartment in Sedona, Arizona. The bathroom will be magnificent! A walk-in shower, a Jacuzzi tub, double vanities—"

He scoops a stray hair from my cheek and stares at me in bewildered wonderment. "Have you been binge-watching some home reno show?"

"So, um, no. It sort of came to me in some kind of full-on vision. That doesn't mean we have to do it. I just thought it was pretty cool."

He leans back and pulls me close. "Sounds good to me. But you know Isadora will be popping in constantly."

Laughter grips me. "You're not wrong."

"Then my only question is, how do we prevent that?"

"I don't know. Maybe I'll talk to Silas. He has a

lot of experience with runes of protection, banishment, and stuff like that. He might have ideas about something we can do to prevent her from blasting through the walls at will."

Erick grins. "If he doesn't come up with anything, I suppose it will be an enter-at-your-own-risk situation. Once we're married, Isadora might get more than she bargains for."

My tummy triple Lutzes with tingles. "What do you mean 'once we're married'? Do you have something planned?"

His eyes sparkle, and once again, the image of a snow princess hits me like a brick wall.

"Erick Harper, if I didn't know better, I might think Silas taught you some kind of trick to block my powers."

His air of superiority falters for a split second, but then the image of the snow princess returns with ferocity. "I have to head into the office on the bright. I should probably call it a night."

My heart sinks. "I didn't take you to be all bark and no *bite*." My eyes dare him to make good on his earlier advances.

He scoops me from the settee in one fluid motion. "I guess you called my bluff, Moon."

"Oops. I guess I did." My attempt to play innocent fails.

He tickles me and tosses me playfully onto the fluffy down comforter.

While he sets an alarm on his phone, I hit the button that drops the blackout shades. He may have to get up at the crack of dawn, but I have no such disorder.

CHAPTER 6

THE HANDY DANDY blackout shades I deployed last
night protect my delicate eyelids from the harsh
rays of the morning sun. When I finally give in and
open my eyes, the pillow next to mine is empty.

If this were a movie, I'd roll over and inhale
deeply! However, this is real life, and I can easily
detect Erick's distinctive woodsy-citrus scent lin-
gering in the surrounding air. Looks like he got that
early start, or the worm, or is getting after life, or
more things like that.

I prefer the approach mentioned on my T-shirt.
A sleeping cat curled into an adorable bundle, followed by the tagline: "Wake me when I run the
world."

I figure winning the grandma lottery and
winding up in a magical place like Pin Cherry

Harbor is about as close to running the world as I'll ever get. And honestly, it's more than enough.

Memories of last night bubble to the surface. Not the salacious kind, the habitation-discussion kind. I tap the speed dial for Silas Willoughby, whom I have listed under *Secret Alchemist* on my phone, and hit speaker while I find the rest of my wardrobe for the day.

"Good morning, Mitzy. To what do I owe the pleasure?"

A tiny voice inside my head reminds me that good manners make a person nice to know. "Good morning, Mr. Willoughby. I would like to discuss my plans for a potential renovation."

"Architecture is one of my favorite hobbies. How can I be of assistance?"

Once I bring him up to speed on my vision-based remodel of the printing museum, I ask the question that truly matters. "So, without offending Grams, are there some alchemical thingamajigs that you can use to sort of keep her from popping in at will?"

His hearty guffaw is hardly the response I want.

"Silas! Be serious. If Erick and I are going to have a life together, we can't be at the whim of a nosy ghost. I mean, I want her in my life, just not whenever she feels like it."

He harrumphs, and I can easily imagine him

smoothing his bushy grey mustache with a thumb and forefinger. "I understand perfectly. You forget how long I knew your grandmother before she transitioned to her ghostly life."

"Touché. I'm sure there are plenty of things about her that you actually know way more about than I do."

There's a tender silence, and his voice is quite emotional when he responds. "In all the years I've known her, I've never seen her as happy as she is with you. You've brought out the best in her, Mitzy. After all the risks we took to ensure that her spirit could remain tethered to your bookshop, I must say, I am most pleased with the outcome."

Now I'm crying. "Silas, I can never repay you for what you've done for my grandmother and me. I hope that me taking my alchemy lessons more seriously and making an effort to give back to my community is a start."

He inhales slowly. "It is more than enough, Mizithra. With regard to your intrusive ghost issues, I am certain we can come up with a workable solution. All I ask is some time to appropriately research the conundrum and assemble one or more feasible solutions."

"Take all the time you need, Silas. All this remodeling stuff is something for my mind to play with to keep me from prying into my boyfriend's brain. I keep thinking Erick is going to propose, but every time we get close to broaching the subject, all I get are images of a *snow princess*."

There's a sharp intake of breath on the other end of the phone, followed by a clairaudient message. *Snow Princess.*

"Silas? I smell a rat, or rather an alchemist in rat's clothing."

He chuckles. "As you may suspect, it is difficult to surprise a psychic. All I can say is the less you know, the happier you shall be."

I knew it! However, I also know exactly how much it means to Erick if he's gone to all of this trouble. "Fine. I promise to mind my manners and wait somewhat patiently while you research my remodeling dilemma."

"You are as gracious as you are intelligent. I thank you, Mizithra."

Oh brother. "Thanks again, Silas. I've got to grab some breakfast and head over to the hospital to see Kurt."

"Kurt? To whom do you refer?"

"Didn't you hear about the fire at the curling club last night?"

"I did not. As you know, I live a fair span outside of town, and I have not yet read the morning paper. Was there any loss of life?"

"As far as I know, Kurt was the only person

trapped inside at the time of the fire. They rescued him, and last I heard, his vitals were strong. I plan to visit him today, just to see if he has any useful information that might help us determine why the curling club was targeted."

Silas harrumphs. "You are familiar with his family history, I assume."

"Grams gave me the bare bones. I hope to learn more when I chat with Kurt. You don't actually think he was involved, do you?"

He sighs. "If one carries a hammer, one tends only to find nails. I bid you adieu, Mizithra."

The call ends, and I'm left half chuckling, half confused. I sort of get the point of the analogy, but Erick always says that everyone's a suspect until they're not. So, I guess I'll try to walk the fine line between only carrying a hammer and keeping everyone on the suspect list. If that's possible?

Today I'll grab a walking breakfast. I won't actually be walking in the freezing cold weather all the way to the hospital, but the term is a throwback to the days before I dropped out of film school.

On set, a walking breakfast is something easy to pick up and carry so that you and the rest of the crew can eat while you work. It's a way to foster goodwill with the crew when they're called to set early. The production company doesn't incur any meal penalties because folks are technically eating, and the crew gets to remain on the clock while they work/eat. Movies are made by efficient crews, and crews run on food. If you mess up meal breaks or cut the budget on craft services—snacks—the movie suffers. I'm not saying that every bad movie that you've ever seen is a result of crappy snack selections, but it's something to think about.

After grabbing a coffee and a chocolate croissant from Bless Choux, I head to the Birch County Regional Medical Facility.

In the big city, strangers are not randomly allowed to visit patients in the hospital. However, in a little town like Pin Cherry, the name Mitzy Moon is well known. Now the reasons for that are not all great, but the receptionist at the main desk recognizes me and calls up to Kurt's room. Lucky for me, he agrees to a visit.

I take the elevator up to the third floor and smile and nod as I make my way down the pale green hallway. As soon as I enter room 323, I know without a doubt I'm in the right place. Kurt's dark eyes and curly brown hair are the spitting image of his mother's.

"Mitzy Moon! Sheriff Harper came by to take my statement this morning, and I wondered when you'd show up."

Not the time to explain that Erick and I don't ship out as a set. "Hi, Kurt. How are you feeling?"

He smiles broadly and gently places a hand on the back of his head. "Aside from the cartoon-sized lump, I'm doing good, you know? My throat hurts from the smoke inhalation, but nothing major. Folks tell me I have you to thank for the rescue."

Oh no. Time to backpedal. "Me? Don't be silly. The firemen were all over that disaster. If anything, we should be thanking Amaryllis. I didn't even know where to find the curling arena."

He smiles and nods.

Hold on. That's my move. Clearly, he's not falling for my self-deprecating reply. Better change the subject. "Do you mind if I ask you some questions about what happened?"

Kurt leans forward eagerly and winces. "Ouch, I moved a little too fast. It sounds like you're taking the case, and I'm afraid that got me a little overexcited."

"Taking the case? So it was arson."

"It was assault, arson, and maybe more, you know? I'm hoping they let me out of here today so I can inspect the damage. See if there's anything missing."

"Missing? Would someone steal curling equipment?"

My comment causes him to burst into laughter. The laughter makes his head throb, and he struggles to subdue it as quickly as possible. "You have to watch the jokes, Miss Moon. Curling stones weigh upwards of forty pounds each. And they're not pricey enough to make the juice worth the squeeze. You'd have to be dumber than a doornail to steal those things."

Not sure whether I should be amused or offended. "Well, you mentioned possible theft. What would they take?"

He inhales sharply. "A few years back, one of our best teams in the history of curling, won the world championship. At the time, they made the trophies from solid gold. Plus, it was technically the first international championship, with all the major countries participating. So the trophy has a lot of historical, as well as actual dollar, value."

"Seriously? A solid-gold curling trophy? How many people know of its existence?"

This question brings another round of painful laughter from the injured Kurt Frazier. "Gee whiz, Miss Moon. My mom always said you were a hoot. But she kinda undersold it, you know? It was an international competition. Everyone in the world knew about it."

Now I'm a little offended. The guy has a head injury, so I'll cut him some slack. "Copy that. Was there any security at the club? Was it kept in a vault or some kind of display case with an alarm system?"

He wags his head from side to side and shrugs.

"The trophy case had Lexan panels instead of glass. Does that count?"

"Not exactly. Are you telling me you had a historically priceless trophy made of solid gold and not so much as a security camera pointed at it? I mean, I don't think you're ever gonna see this thing again."

Kurt's bemused expression vanishes. "Oh please, Miss Moon. Tell me you're joking. I need this job—bad. If that trophy— It took a lot for me to get hired. Because of my dad—"

I put up a hand and wave his worries away. "Listen, Kurt; I didn't mean to sound as though I'd given up. You don't have to talk to me about family. The Duncans have their own history."

He nods knowingly. "Hey, your grandpa, Cal Duncan, was on the winning team."

"Wow. It's true. You do learn something new every day. Well, I'm officially on the case. I'll do everything in my power to find out who set fire to the arena. And once you're back on your feet and have a chance to take a look at the facility, you let me know if that trophy is missing."

He nods his head and grimaces. "Yeah, I'll do that. Just as soon as my head stops throbbing, you know?"

"Yeah, the most important thing is to take care of yourself, Kurt. I'm sure your mom would agree with me."

He chuckles softly. "You have no idea."

As I walk toward the elevator, a sharp pain grips my heart. Maybe I *don't* have any idea. With my mother passing away when I was eleven, I never had to deal with her truly guilt-tripping me with worry, and she never experienced adult Mitzy Moon getting into trouble. Although, Grams and Pyewacket have certainly done more than their fair share of worrying about me. So I suppose I have a bit of an idea.

CHAPTER 7

WITHOUT CONSCIOUSLY CHOOSING A DIRECTION, I find myself parked in front of the sheriff's station. At first, the assumption is my heart must have led me to my boyfriend's place of work. However, as I hop out of the Jeep and head for the front door, Kurt's comment about Erick taking his statement pops to the forefront.

There's got to be a reason that's supposed to make sense. I'll check the story he gave me against the story he gave Erick. If I'm truly on the case, I have to follow up every lead.

When I push through the front door, the deputy I've nicknamed Furious Monkeys, shockingly, looks up from the game on her phone. "Hiya, Mitzy. Are you here to see Sheriff Harper?"

The eye contact and friendly tone throw me off. "Um, yes. Aren't you playing your game?"

She throws her head back in exasperation. "I wish! I beat the last level before breakfast. There's supposed to be an update coming out today, but it's been delayed. I don't know what to do with myself." Deputy Baird grips the phone and shakes it as though the motion could trigger the awaited update.

I'd love to point out that she could try doing her job, but that seems unnecessarily rude. "I hope the update comes through soon. Is it all right if I head back?"

Baird smiles. "You don't have to ask. He's always in a better mood after he sees you." She tilts her head toward the crooked wooden gate, and I grin as I push through.

Deputy Johnson is the only officer in the bullpen, and he's tapping away on his typewriter with serious focus. He doesn't look up when I pass.

When I round the corner into Erick's office, the ever-present mountain of paperwork appears unchanged.

He looks up and grins broadly. "What, no pastries?"

The high from Deputy Baird's compliment vanishes, and my shoulders droop. "Sorry. I came straight from the hospital."

Leaning back, he laces his fingers together behind his head and sucks a breath between his teeth. "I was hoping you were going to steer clear of this one. The fire department seriously suspects arson. Updated me this morning. So far, no traces of accelerant, but with the lump on the back of Kurt's head, they know someone else was in the building."

Nodding slowly, I take a seat in one of the uncomfortable scarred wooden chairs meant to keep visitors from overstaying their welcome. "I'm sort of obligated. Kurt wants me to take the case. He's had to overcome a lot of misconceptions. I'm sure you know all about his father."

Erick exhales and leans forward. His expression is serious, bordering on grim. "It's a reputation that his father deserves. And if someone is willing to burn down an arena with someone inside, we're not dealing with teenage vandals."

"Vandals? Was that actually someone's working theory?"

"Look, Moon, we don't all have psychic senses to fall back on. We have to follow the evidence. Broken windows, spray-painted tags, and an inexplicable fire. Generally, that adds up to vandals. The fact that whoever did this was willing to trap Kurt inside . . . That changes my opinion."

"Good. How soon can Kurt get into the facility to check the inventory?"

Sheriff Harper blinks and stares. "Inventory?

What are you talking about? I don't think the fire department is going to let anyone back on site."

"Oh. Didn't Kurt tell you about the chance there was a theft?"

His jaw muscles tighten. "He did not. I'd appreciate it if you'd share this new information."

Weird. Why would Kurt tell me about a possible theft and not mention it to law enforcement? Seems kinda sketchy. "Maybe he wanted to be sure before he made an official report. He only mentioned it to me in passing, and it wasn't like he was certain anything had been taken."

Erick shakes his head. "Even teenagers wouldn't be desperate enough to steal curling equipment. It's—"

"I know. It's heavy and not worth the effort."

He nods. "So what did Kurt tell you?"

I relay the story about the championship game and the gold trophy. As I mention my grandfather having been a member of the team, the old black-and-white photo Pyewacket passed off earlier pops into my psychic recall. "There's a picture—the picture Pye gave me earlier. It was taken in front of a trophy case. The gold curling stone trophy was in the case. Do you think the fire chief would be willing to let us examine the contents? If that thing is missing, the sooner we start looking for it, the better, right?"

Erick calmly rises from his creaky chair and walks around the desk. He crosses his arms over his chest in that yummy way that makes his biceps bulge. However, the look on his face is no invitation. "I'm officially asking you to back away from this, Moon. There's no need to risk civilians where this case is involved. If you bring the photo down to the station, I'll talk to the fire chief and see if I can take a look at the trophy case—or what's left of it."

I've never been great with authority, and I'm especially bothered when my boyfriend tries to boss me around. Getting to my feet, I attempt to make myself taller than I am. I still have to look up into the ice-blue eyes of the sheriff, but my tone clearly indicates I'm not about to back down. "My photo. My evidence."

That muscle in his jaw clenches once again. "This." He points to my person. "This is one of the biggest things standing between us."

For a split second, the image of the snow princess hangs in the ether. But it vanishes without a trace.

"Do you mean me? This is what I do. I help people who need help. How is that standing between us?"

He chews the inside of his cheek, and I can feel the tension in the room growing. "I shouldn't have to repeat myself. But I will. I've never encouraged you to put yourself in danger by poking around my crime scenes. If we were married, it wouldn't be appropriate. I hold an elected position in Birch County. Paulsen came incredibly close to beating me in the last election. She's a great deputy, but it would be very easy for her to stir up trouble if my *wife* were to run around breaking laws and illegally accessing crime scenes. I have my job to think about."

I hadn't heard how close the election was, but the unspoken accusation is that my public interference with investigations was the tide that turned some voters to Paulsen's camp at the polls. "I'm not sure I appreciate the implication, Sheriff."

He shakes his head and steps back. "I'll send Deputy Johnson by to collect the photo. Withholding evidence or interfering with an investigation is a crime punishable by not more than ninety days in jail."

My eyes widen. I can't believe he's taking this seriously. In the past— What the heck is happening? "Are you breaking up with me?"

His face shifts to panic, and remorse rolls off him in waves. "Of course not. But I have to put my foot down. I can't do my job properly if I'm constantly worried about something terrible happening to you. I'm not trying to tell you what to do, Mitzy." He reaches out and tenderly grips my hands. "I love you. When I'm preoccupied with worry, I'm not a good sheriff. There are so many other great things you've done for this community, and I'm sure there are plenty of additional opportunities. I'm only encouraging you to shift your focus toward those and leave the whole crime-solving thing to me. Can't you understand?"

On the surface, his comments seem innocent and totally understandable. However, I've never made a secret of who I am. Ever since he met me, I've been taking risks and solving cases. Five years ago, back in Arizona, I never would've seen myself doing this or even imagined I could enjoy it. Now, after everything I've been through, it feels like this is what I was meant to do. It defines me. How can he expect me to give up the very essence of who I am?

Sudden pressure on my hands pulls me from a potential shame spiral.

"Mitzy, I know that look. Where did you go?"

"I'm going back to my apartment. Maybe we'll talk about this later. But right now, I need to be alone." Pulling my hand from his, I step toward the door. It hurts me to my core to see the look of pain flash through his eyes.

Silently walking out of the station, I'm still not exactly sure what happened. News of his mother's plans to relocate and Mr. Willoughby's willingness to help me corral my maverick Ghost-ma all seemed like positive signs. But this debate about who should be doing what and the implication that my cavalier attitude is threatening his livelihood— Well, this could be the straw that breaks the camel's back. Or is it too many cooks in the kitchen spoiling the broth?

Anyway, the ookey feeling in my stomach does not bode well.

CHAPTER 8

THE SHORT DRIVE back to my bookshop gives me precious little time to fume. Grams is definitely going to hear about this latest development in the saga that is my personal life. If only Twiggy were in town! I can almost hear her cackle echoing from the remote Fijian island where she and Wayne chose to spend the holidays.

The metal alleyway door slams behind me, and I call out loudly. "Grams! Grams, where are you?"

"I regret to inform you I have not communicated with your grandmother as of yet. Although, my time in the Rare Books Loft has prevented me from overtly seeking her company."

The calm voice of my mentor bounces off the tin-plated ceilings and quickly dampens my anger. The "Closed for the Holidays" sign in the front window never applies to Silas. He has his own key —for this very reason.

Wandering past the stacks, I call out, "Hey, Silas. I didn't know you were coming into town today. What are you up to?"

He harrumphs. His bald head, bushy mustache, and frumpy tweed coat appear at the top of the spiral staircase as he leans against the balustrade. "Of the two of us, I would assume my advanced age would result in more memory loss than yours. Is it possible that you have already forgotten our recent conversation?"

Oops. "Right. Researching the ghost blocker. Yeesh. Sorry. I guess I'm distracted."

He motions for me to join him on the mezzanine and disappears from view. I gingerly step over the chain and tromp up to the second-floor loft.

"Please have a seat, Mizithra. Agitation is interfering with your abilities. Have you also forgotten the tools I've shared with you for finding a calm center?"

His wisdom and tone always tend to leave me feeling as though I'm a small child being scolded by the headmaster.

"No. I had a fight with Erick. I mean, it wasn't even really a fight. He sort of gave me an ultimatum. I don't know. It was all so confusing and frustrating."

Silas leans back and places a hand on his round belly. He takes three deep breaths and continues. "Relationships are fraught with complication. Each is a unique and delicate dance. There must be give and take, yet there must also be support. The hardest thing for an independent woman, such as you, is to allow herself to be vulnerable. After your mother's passing, your years in foster care forced you to be self-sufficient. After forming such a strong core, it must be difficult to accept the help of others."

"I wish that was it. Erick's not offering to help. He's pretty much insisting that I stop my amateur sleuthing immediately. In fact, it's kind of sounding like I have to choose between being his wife or being who I am."

Silas wipes a hand across his bald pate and gazes into the middle distance. "Repeat the conversation. Verbatim."

I open my mouth to protest, but then the power of psychic recall raises its hand like a student in Mr. Kotter's class. I may not consciously remember exactly what Erick said, but using this ability that Silas helped me refine, I can play the entire conversation back like a movie. Pausing or fast-forwarding when necessary. Playing the clip, I recite the dialogue.

The facial expression of my alchemical mentor

does not change. However, he makes an occasional grumble, sigh, or grunt of agreement. After I've shared all the details, he calmly continues to stare into space.

"Well? What do you think? It's an ultimatum, right?"

Silas smooths his mustache with a thumb and forefinger. "One of the most difficult things in life is to place ourselves in the boots of another. You experience life through your own eyes. Your reactions are based on your own past. Imagine, for a moment, what it must be like to experience these events as Erick Harper."

I can't stop my eyes from rolling, but I reluctantly agree. "All right."

Initially, it seems a straightforward exercise. Not that long ago, I literally found myself in Erick's shoes, but the switcheroo is another story.

Closing my eyes, I imagine being Erick. To say that my efforts are lackluster is an understatement.

A moment later, my eyelids pop open, and I shrug. "Is he embarrassed because I'm solving his cases? He knows about my powers now. Erick knows I have an advantage."

Silas nods thoughtfully and waits. He steeples his fingers and patiently bounces his chin on the tip of his pointers.

I knew it! This is a lesson. I attempt some additional Erick-ing, but nothing makes sense. He isn't the kind of guy who is easily embarrassed. And he knows— Wait!

He might know, but everyone else *doesn't* know. Deputy Paulsen is a stickler for rules, regulations, and letting the sheriff's department handle everything. It wouldn't surprise me if she made my flaunting of said rules part of her official campaign. Honestly, I have no idea since I simply went directly to the polls and voted for Erick. I didn't review her pamphlets, and I consciously avoided looking at any of her posted campaign signs when driving around town. Not for a second did I consider voting for her.

"Silas, do you think I *am* actually endangering Erick's job?"

His head neither nods nor shakes. It makes more of a noncommittal circle. "Actions are open to interpretation. Those interpretations are colored by the examiner. Erick mentioned Deputy Paulsen, and I believe we know her to be somewhat judgmental when it comes to your interferences."

"Somewhat! You must be joking. Some days, I think she actually hates me. If she could use my actions against Erick, I would never forgive myself."

Silas returns to bouncing his chin on his fingertips.

"But— I actually like solving these puzzles. Before arriving in Pin Cherry, I worked a bunch of brainless dead-end jobs. Nothing ever challenged me, and I always felt like a failure. When I solve these cases, bring criminals to justice, and help the victims or the victims' families, I feel useful. Are you saying I should give all of that up to be some kind of Stepford wife?"

At long last, Silas stops the bouncing and fixes me with a wizened stare. "Relationships in which one party abandons their passion in favor of pleasing the other never end well. Both people must feel joy."

An enormous sigh deflates my chest. "I love everything about Erick. I don't want him to change. Why does he expect me to?"

Silas offers a fatherly nod. "I believe this is what couples commonly refer to as a difficult conversation. Your love for Erick cannot change reality any more than his love for you could. Somewhere in the midst of this confusion lies a solution. Perhaps each party may have to give more than they imagine. Perhaps not. Until you broach the subject with clear intention, the universe can hardly be bothered to offer you options."

"What do you mean? Are you saying that the powers that be are withholding an answer because I'm difficult?"

He chuckles and smooths his mustache. "I'm

sure you have heard the saying, 'when the student is ready, the teacher appears.' It is similar with everyday problems. Until you sharpen your focus and define the problem which needs resolution, you are unlikely to uncover the solution."

Leaning back, I groan in defeat, and my shoulders sag. "Yeah, that makes sense. Looks like we'll be having the talk."

Silas nods and returns to his research. The lesson and the conversation have ended.

Walking toward the bookcase, I reach up with my left hand and tilt the candle sconce that activates the secret door.

Pyewacket is stretched across the four-poster and yawns widely as I approach.

Flopping onto the thick down comforter beside him, I stroke the rough fur between his ears and beg for sympathy. "You're on my side, right, buddy? Erick isn't the boss of me, right?"

"Ree-ow." Soft but condescending.

Rolling onto my back, I kick my feet in the air like a toddler having a tantrum. "Fine. No one is the boss of anyone. I get it. Compromise. Give and take. Blah. Blah. Blah."

"Reow." Can confirm.

"How'd you get so smart, son?" As I scratch my fingers along his spine, a sense of knowing lifts the hairs on the back of my neck. "You're more than just a cat, aren't you?"

His large golden eyes fix me with a piercing stare.

I can see worlds within those orbs. Time passes differently for this magnificent creature.

Robin Pyewacket Goodfellow pushes a large paw in my direction. Under the retracted claws lies a photo. The photo of my grandfather and the trophy case.

"Oh, Mr. Cuddlekins, our moment has passed, hasn't it?"

He squeezes his eyelids closed dismissively, and I rise with a sigh. "Time for me to get back to solving the case." As I walk toward the arson wall to tack up the image, a flash of conscience hits me.

On second thought, I'm going to take this photograph to Erick. Hopefully, he'll see it as the peace offering it's intended to be.

"Thanks for the therapy sesh, Pye. Put it on my tab."

Silence.

A smug, superior silence.

CHAPTER 9

MY RETURN to the sheriff's station is far from triumphant. The smile that graced Furious Monkeys' face earlier is long gone. She frowns and shakes her head. "I don't know what you said to him, but he was not happy. He left a few minutes ago in a huff. Mumbled something about needing to clear his head."

Looks like my day has taken an unwelcome turn. Smiling weakly, I attempt to trade on our earlier rapport. "Did he happen to say where he was going?"

I sense her internal struggle. She has her boss's best interests at heart, and right now, she's clearly not sure if I'm one of those.

"He may have mentioned something about the

arena." She gazes at me pleadingly. "But you didn't hear it from me, okay?"

"10-4."

With that, I drive toward the charred remains of the once glorious fieldhouse ice arena. In the daylight, the scene is quite gruesome. The blackened building stands out starkly against the distant mounds of pristine snow heaped on the frozen great lake. While the immediate area surrounding the former hockey rink is a sludgy, frozen mess of grey and black slush.

The only car in the parking lot is the sheriff's cruiser. I park next to it, confirm it's empty, and head toward the burned-out building.

Bright yellow crime scene tape stretches over broken windows and shattered doors.

After this morning's hoopla, I better mind my manners. "Erick? Erick, are you in there?"

No reply.

Well, I never said I was a saint.

Lifting the yellow tape, I duck under and pick my way through the ashes. The choking aroma of melted plastic and charred wood leaves an unpleasant aftertaste in my mouth. The sooner I find Erick, the better.

My five regular senses aren't going to cut it. A quick check-in with my special abilities helps me identify a route toward the hallway that once contained a trophy case and maybe still does.

When I turn the final corner, Erick is so distracted by his thoughts he doesn't hear me coming. He has one hand on the sooty wall and the other covering his face. If I were psychic—and I am—it seems like he might be dealing with some super personal emotions.

I'd love to tiptoe away and pretend I never saw this, but, with my clumsy luck, I'll trip over something and get caught in the middle of my attempted escape.

"Erick?" My soft voice seems like a shout in the silence.

He spins on a dime and swipes angrily at his face. "Moon? What in—?"

Holding the picture aloft, I put both of my hands in the air as though it were a Wild West stickup. "I come in peace. I wanted to give you the photo. No strings attached. You weren't at the station, so I figured—"

Exhaling in defeat, he strides toward me. His long legs swallow up the distance in seconds, and he scoops his arms around me and kisses me passionately.

The taste of salty tears on his lips breaks my heart. "I don't want to fight. And I don't want to jeopardize your job."

Erick tucks a wild strand of white hair under my crooked stocking hat and attempts a smile. "Sorry I snapped at you earlier. This fire really got under my skin—and clipped a foot or two off my fuse. If my abilities as a sheriff are so fragile that a concerned citizen helping victims' families could ruin my whole career— Then it might be time for me to look for a new calling."

Circling my arms tightly around him, I squeeze with all my heart. I can't believe I ever doubted this amazing man. "I'm sure there's a middle ground. I can try harder to follow rules, and—"

His gentle kiss interrupts my attempted soliloquy. "Look, Moon, I love you exactly the way you are. I was totally out of line earlier. We can figure this out. If history has taught me anything, it's that we're a great team."

"You mean, like a power couple?"

He chuckles. "Not exactly. When we work together on cases, everyone benefits. If Paulsen can't see that, then nothing I do will change her mind."

"You don't have to tell me twice. She's about as stubborn as a—"

"Mitzy Moon?" Erick arches an eyebrow and smirks.

We share a chuckle, and he kisses my forehead. The official signal that our argument is over, or at least on hiatus.

Erick exhales with force and stretches his head from side to side. "Now, let's put those psychic senses of yours to work. The trophy case survived because it's made from Lexan. It's blackened on the outside, but it didn't break or shatter like standard glass would have. Some of the cheaper plastic trophies are dust, rather puddles, but most survived. Still, there may be something missing. Can I see the photo?"

"Absolutely, Sheriff. This is your investigation, and you should have all the evidence you need." Handing him the photo, I curtsy and bow.

He grins and comically slumps his shoulders. "Okay, Moon, you made your point. There's no need to patronize me."

Before he has a chance to scan the photo, I blurt, "It's missing. Erick, look!" Pointing to the trophy behind my grandfather's left shoulder, I continue, "That's the world championship trophy, right? The one made of gold?"

Erick traces his finger across the photo as his eyes scan the case. "Yeah, that's the one. And it is definitely not here. Looks like I better head back over to the hospital and see if Kurt would like to amend his statement. It's so strange . . . I still can't figure out why he didn't tell me in the first place."

"He did have a concussion. Plus, at least he told me. And since we're a team—"

Sheriff Harper smiles and takes my hand. "I'll walk you back to your car, young lady. It's not safe to be in this building." He takes a few small steps, gently tugs me along, and then stops cold. "Honestly, you might be rubbing off on me, though. I didn't even clear my visit with the fire chief."

I lean away and glance up at him in mock horror. "Oh, dear! From sheriff to bad boy in the blink of an eye."

As we step through what once served as the front door onto the blackened slush, Erick scoops an arm around my waist and pulls me close. "I'd like to show you a bit more of the bad boy later. How's your schedule lookin'?"

And I'm dead! After a shuddering breath and a moment to compose myself, I'm able to answer. "I hope you don't think it's getting the cart ahead of the horse, but I have a meeting with an architect later. Could you get away and join us?"

He stares, expressionless.

"Oh brother, this is silly. I should cancel, shouldn't I?"

"Absolutely not. I loved your ideas. The layout you talked about sounds great. I'd like to be involved in choosing the finishes, if that's the right term."

A huge smile creeps across my face. "Choosing the finishes! Wow, I had no idea you were a home-makeover addict." Fanning myself with a sooty mitten, I can't hide my giggles.

He pulls me toward the parking lot. "I watch some television with my mom when I find the time. So, I have some opinions about tile and paint color. But nothing too crazy."

"No problem. If you're free, the architect is supposed to swing by the bookshop around 4:00 or 4:30. I'd love to have your input."

He helps me into the Jeep, leans against the door, and flashes his baby blues. "If I can get Kurt's revised statement, get the reports updated, and assign a deputy to investigate the theft, maybe I'll knock off early and bring some takeout. Sweet-and-sour chicken?"

"You know me too well, Sheriff."

His easy laugh is the only sign I need that things are almost back to all right between us.

He jumps into his vehicle, and I obediently follow him out of the parking lot. I'd love to poke around the arena a bit longer, but it would be a bad choice to instantly destroy the good will I just built.

Best head back to home base and update the team. If we're in search of gold, Grams will be first in line with ideas!

CHAPTER 10

TURNS OUT PLANS TO REMODEL are much higher on Ghost-ma's priority list than gold rushes.

"Grams, are you one hundred percent sure you're okay with donating all the printing artifacts?"

She smiles wistfully and circles the massive chandelier suspended above the stacks in the main bookshop. "Oh, you know me, dear. The novelty wore off after a year or two, but the local Parent Teacher Association insisted it was a necessary field trip locale."

"I can't remember a single class coming through since I arrived in town. Well, maybe a couple—but it's no hot spot. Seems like times they are a-changin', Isadora."

"I absolutely agree, sweetie. But I'll need a new

place to work on my—your—memoirs." She ghost coughs in an attempt to distract me from the mention of her intrusive writing project.

My eyes roll of their own accord. "Right. I can put a desk in the apartment. Once Erick and I officially move into the new digs, I'll only be visiting the apartment out of nostalgia."

"What? What about all the clothes? Will your new closet do them justice? Currently, you have built-in shoe racks and—"

"I tell you what, why don't I leave all the high-fashion pieces exactly where they're at? I'll take a few items to my new closet, but I'll keep that more minimalist. And I'll be sharing with Erick."

Grams falls from the ceiling like a stone dropped from the Empire State building. "Sharing a closet! What is the world coming to?"

"Spare me the dramatics, Isadora. I'll still have the entire apartment closet to myself. If there are any special occasions, or undercover assignments, that require wardrobe assistance, you and I will have this place all to ourselves."

Ghost-ma glides back and forth anxiously and shakes her shimmering head. "Well, I suppose two closets are better than one shared closet. But I can pop into your new closet to help pick out clothes anytime."

It takes some quick mental shenanigans on my

part to close off the conversation I had with Silas and think of other things before Grams can perform her usual intrusive thought-dropping.

"Intrusive thought-dropping! Well, I don't know what you're hiding from me, but I'm already not a fan of this remodel. You should be nicer to the resident ghost, dear. I could certainly stir up more than a little trouble by haunting the workmen."

Placing a fist on my curvy hip, I narrow my gaze and lower my voice. "Listen, Myrtle Isadora; there will be no haunting of workmen, architects, interior designers, or anyone else. If you want free rein planning my wedding, then you will be very careful who you threaten in this bookshop."

My extrasensory perceptions pick up on the mounting tsunami of resistance. However, to my grandmother's credit, she swallows her pride and acquiesces. "I'm sure we'll all have to make sacrifices and adjustments to accommodate the new living arrangements. I just want to be clear. I was here first." She crosses her arms, and her perfectly coral bottom lip juts out.

I flash my eyebrows and snicker. "Don't worry, we all know who is queen of the Bell, Book & Candle."

No sooner have the words passed through my lips than the self-appointed king of the bookshop slinks down the circular staircase and makes his demands known.

"RE-ow." Feed me.

"As you wish, m'lord."

Grams runs her ethereal fingers along Pyewacket's back, and he curves his spine in response. "I need to get my things organized, Mitzy. How soon do you think they'll start the renovation?"

"No idea. I'm meeting with the architects this afternoon, and we'll see what kind of schedule they propose. I'm sure there will be plenty of time. I was hoping to wait until Twiggy got back from her vacation and put her to work on clearing out the museum."

Grams taps a manicured finger against her coral lips. "Good idea. Everyone playing to their strengths. That's the best way forward."

Covering my mouth with one hand, I hide my grin. "By the way, you're welcome to observe my meeting with the architect, but if you stir up any trouble—"

Ghost-ma traces a finger in an "X" over her bosom. "Cross my heart and hope to die—well, leave this plane. I will mind my manners. I know what you'll do to my couture if I break my promise."

"Wonderful. Then we have an accord." I bow deeply and flourish my hand.

She laughs until she ghost snorts and vanishes through the wall.

A call from an unknown number is almost unheard of in Pin Cherry. I toy with the idea of letting it go to voicemail in case it's some ridiculous telemarketer trying to sell me an extended warranty on my vehicle! Luckily, my psychic senses nudge me, and I grab the call.

Artie proceeds to bring me up to speed on Kurt's situation and asks if the two of them can swing by the bookshop and pick me up on their way to the arena.

"Sure. I've got about an hour before my meeting. That should give us enough time, right?"

She confirms and ends the call. A couple of minutes later, a sharp knock on the side door announces their arrival. Tugging my hat down snuggly, I step into the alley and wave. Artie heads back to the driver's seat and motions for me to hop into the middle of her old truck's bench seat. Kurt steps out to allow me access.

"Hey, Kurt. Good to see you out of the hospital." I climb into the middle spot and angle my knees away from the "four on the floor" shifter.

He gingerly nods and gets in the truck. "Yeah, it's good to be out. There's nothing relaxing about nurses coming in every couple of hours, poking and prodding me. They released me on the condition I stay with my mom for a couple days, and they won't clear me to drive until I come back for a follow-up."

"Makes sense. Have you been able to remember anything else about the events leading up to the fire?"

"Nothing. They must've hit me from behind. I never saw it coming."

Artie jumps into the conversation. "It's a real shame, you know. That ice rink, and the curling club, provided a lot of healthy distraction for young people in this community. I can't imagine all the trouble those kids will be gettin' up to now."

Huh? It never occurred to me that the hockey rink and some bowling alleys made from ice could be that important to Pin Cherry Harbor. Sounds like something the Duncan-Moon Philanthropic Foundation should look into. Maybe I'll chat with my dad later. Since Cal was a member of that championship team, it only seems fair to give Jacob the opportunity to get involved too.

"If you think of anything, Kurt, even the smallest detail. It could help."

Artie turns into the now familiar parking lot, and Kurt gasps. "Whoa! That fire really got out of control."

His mother grumbles her reluctant agreement. "Yup. If I hadn't called the paramedics when I did—"

My psychic senses tingle, and my mood ring re-plays the image of Kurt calling out for help.

"Hold on. You were on the phone with your mother? Were you conscious when you were trapped in the storeroom?"

A faint ripple of defensiveness hits me in the gut

Kurt gazes out the passenger-side window. "It's all pretty fuzzy. I think I called my mom to see what was for dinner. I don't remember the rest."

It's possible the ring is showing me the scene as a reminder of what led Amaryllis and me to the rink. Hmmmm. Something doesn't add up.

"So, you were on the phone with your mom. What do you remember, Artie?"

She nods in agreement with Kurt. "Well, you know. We were chatting about the roast I had in the oven. Then he kinda groaned, and there was a crash." Artie puts the truck in first gear, turns off the engine, and stomps the e-brake to the floor. "I figured maybe he tripped and dropped his phone. But he never picked it up. I called out, and there was nothing. Just radio silence."

Interesting. She knew he was at the arena when she called the paramedics, but she didn't know about the fire. "Kurt, when do you remember regaining consciousness? Did you try to get out of the room when you woke up?"

He gently touches the lump on the back of his head and flinches. "I don't know. Maybe. It's all a blur, Mitzy. If I woke up, I'm sure I tried to get out. I don't remember anything until I woke up in the hospital."

I'll make a mental note to check with Erick if the firemen found the door locked or barricaded in some way. "Well, let's head inside and see what we find." For now, I plan to keep it to myself that I made an earlier trip. Erick and I aren't as familiar with the facility as Kurt must be. I don't want to say anything that may lead him down one path or another. I'd much prefer to hear his recollection of things as they were before the fire.

The three of us trudge through the dirty slush, duck under the crime scene tape, and carefully pick our way through the rubble. I pull my shirt up over my mouth to cut some of the smoky stench.

Kurt is mostly silent, aside from an occasional woeful grunt as he surveys the horrible scene, and what remains of the nonsense "tags" sprayed on the walls.

His mother attempts to keep her tone upbeat. "What should we look for, Kurt?"

"Let's check the trophy case first. Then we can see if the equipment room survived, and the Zamboni garage."

I give his shoulder a supportive squeeze. "Sounds good. You lead the way."

He turns down the hallway that I now know houses the trophy case. Kurt glances at the un-broken but sooty Lexan and pulls a sharp breath between his teeth. "It's gone! The gold trophy . . . Someone must've stolen it during the fire, or maybe since." He paces anxiously, and his hands ball into fists.

"I'm so sorry, Kurt. This isn't your fault. We'll find the trophy. I'm sure of it." There's a strange vibe under the surface of Kurt's reaction. Hopefully, my fake reassuring tone is convincing.

He looks at me and offers a disbelieving smile. "This way to the equipment rooms."

I follow as he goes through the motions of checking the equipment rooms, locker rooms, and Zamboni garage. There's smoke damage, water damage, and plenty of burned remains. But most of the important things seem intact.

Artie leads the way back to the car. "Well, that's a load off, eh, Kurt? All the equipment accounted for, and the Zamboni in good order. Probably some vandals, like you suspected. I bet Sheriff Harper will have those good-for-nothing kids and that trophy rounded up in no time."

Far be it from me to point out that Kurt is clearly hiding something. Only a mother's love could ignore the nervous energy pulsing through Kurt Frazier as we drive away.

"You can drop me at the corner, Artie." Kurt slides out of the truck and offers me a hand exiting the vehicle.

My psychic senses pick up on a brief flicker of deception. He's hiding something. Right now, I can't put my finger on it, but it's worth noting.

"Thanks for the call, Artie." I smile and wave. "If you happen to think of anything else, Kurt, a smell, a sound, anything—your mom has my number."

He smiles, but it doesn't touch his eyes. "Thanks, Mitzy. I definitely will do that."

Kurt climbs into the truck, and they drive off down First Avenue.

I'd love to run down to the sheriff's station and share my concerns with Erick, but there's no time before my appointment.

Removing the hefty brass key that I carry on a chain under my shirt, I insert the odd triangle-shaped barrel into the lock in the hand-carved door. Gazing at the mythical images adorning the golden-brown wood, Pyewacket's recent reincarnation sparks curiosity.

I've always thought the image of the cat carved in the door resembled Pyewacket. Right down to the scratches over his left eye. As far as anyone can tell me, this door was carved over three hundred years ago. Silas found it during a trip to Mexico and had it shipped to almost-Canada as a grand-opening gift for my grandmother's bookshop.

I always doubted the story. I assumed they were playing tricks on me or purposely keeping Pyewacket's origins mystical. However, after his most recent stunt and the strange psychic message earlier, I wonder if he truly could be centuries old.

What if he is? Has he helped other humans? Are there distant relatives in my family tree that have served the same furry master?

Snap out of it, Mitzy! There's no time for an existential crisis.

CHAPTER 11

SINCE I'M EXPECTING the architects, I leave the front door unlocked and hurry upstairs to swap out my snarky T-shirt for a somewhat more professional sweater.

The bookstore is eerily quiet. Without Twiggy to boss me around or cackle at my mishaps, and with Grams tucked away on the third floor of the museum sorting through her massive writing project, the place seems twice as large as usual.

It will be nice to welcome Erick into this space. Well, the other space. The new space—after it's remodeled.

Once again, my mind movies steal precious minutes. I'm struggling to yank a sweater over my head when a voice calls up from the first floor.

"Miss Moon? Mitzy Moon? There doesn't seem to be anyone here. I have an appointment."

The last thing I want to do is get off on the wrong foot with the person or persons who will be helping my vision become reality.

I force my head through the tight neck opening, rake my fingers through my messy white hair, and run across the Rare Books Loft.

From the top of the spiral staircase, I call, "Hello! I'm Mitzy. I'll be right down. We'll be heading into the adjacent space. Give me one second." Hustling down the spiral staircase, I risk unhooking the chain.

My fingers sweat as I struggle to hook it back in place before the thirty-second window expires and sirens literally wail.

Success!

The thrill of beating the clock places a too-friendly grin on my façade.

"Good afternoon, Miss Moon. I'm Sophia Lari. I'm looking forward to getting a feel for the space and showing you my ideas."

Hmmmm. I'm not sure I appreciate the emphasis on MY, being her, ideas.

Blerg. Looks like it's just the one "person." Nothing like an over-eager architect who already plans on ignoring the owner's suggestions.

Struggling to keep the mask in place, I feign excitement. "Wonderful. Let me text my boyfriend real quick. He may be joining us."

The architect smiles, pulls her phone from her tote bag, and pretends to listen to her messages.

I can assure you it *is* all pretend. Let's remember; I have more than your basic senses at work here.

A quick text to Erick confirms he's only steps from the front door.

He stomps the slush off his boots on the doormat and calls out. "Mitzy? Are you still on this side of the door?"

"You're just in time. We're headed into the museum now."

Sophia drops her message-less phone back into her tote and steps to the side.

I depress the push bar on the "Employees Only" door and flick on all the lighting. "Follow me."

Erick and Ms. Lari cross the threshold.

She gazes around the vast space and offers an obligatory compliment. "Wonderful bones. I'm excited about getting started."

Smile and nod, like my mother taught me. "Great. Here, on the main floor, I want to keep it very open plan. With a large kitchen, dining room, and cozy fireplace with plenty of seating in the living room."

Sophia Lari isn't taking any notes. She's nodding as though she's listening, but I sense her attention has wandered. Her comment confirms my suspicion.

"It would be wonderful to juxtapose an ultra-modern kitchen with this exposed brick. You could paint everything white, and have a large island with waterfall marble counters . . ."

My eyes seek out Erick. His face is scrunched up with concern, and I arch my eyebrow in solidarity as I reply, "That's very interesting. Although, ultra-modern isn't really our style. We'd like to keep things a little more homey, and preserve as much of the building's historic beauty as possible."

She takes a breath but charges ahead with her own vision. "Based on what I saw in the bookshop, I feel confident that you've already checked all the boxes necessary for the historical society. We can do most of these renovations without a permit, and—"

Thankfully, Erick jumps in and extends his hand. "Excuse me, I didn't catch your name. Sheriff Harper here. You can call me Erick. I definitely want to make sure everything we do during the renovation is properly permitted." He points to the badge and smiles. "I'm sure you understand."

Sophia shakes his outstretched hand and, to her credit, doesn't even blush at her faux pas. "No, of course. There's more than one way to skin a cat, Sheriff."

Somewhere in the bookshop, a caracal hisses loudly.

"By the way, my name is Sophia Lari. I don't think you were here when I introduced myself. I promise to take great care of this project. Sometimes it's difficult for clients to get out of their own heads. It may sound strange to move things in a modern direction, but you'll love the end result."

Wow! This chick really isn't reading the room. Time to use one of the techniques I've previously only practiced with Silas.

Taking a deep breath, I focus on my vision for the remodel, honing in on every last detail. Then I send that vision to Sophia. Technically, it's as easy as attaching a photo to an email. Although it requires a level of psychic ability I've only recently come to master. I can send images to Silas with zero difficulty. Sending it to someone with no paranormal feelers and heavily guarded preconceived notions may be beyond my reach. Regardless, I give it the old college try.

Ms. Lari stops mid-sentence and blinks. Thin fingers rub sharply at her left temple, and she shakes her head as though attempting to dislodge water from her inner ear.

Erick glances my way and shrugs.

I grin and wink.

Sophia Lari pulls a bottle of designer water from her handbag and takes a long sip. "Goodness. I felt a headache coming on for a moment there, but I'm fine now. Where was I? Oh, right. Large kitchen, open plan, and a fireplace in that corner. What do you think?"

Sheriff Harper tilts his head and his gaze shifts from concern to accusation. Before he can point the finger at me, I jump onto Sophia's last suggestion. "Perfect. That actually sounds amazing."

He shakes his head and refuses to be part of whatever he imagines I've done.

My goal is to keep this party moving and get Ms. Lari to wrap up the walk-through before she realizes I've supplanted my vision for hers.

We head up to the second floor, and things continue without a hitch. When we reach the third floor, I feel quite pleased with the way things are going.

Right up until—

Sophia Lari screams, points, and faints dead away!

Erick, always quick on his feet, catches her before she hits the floor.

"Grams! What did I tell you? You literally scared this woman to death—or at least to faint!"

Isadora drops her quill pen and stares in disbelief. "My goodness! I didn't even hear you coming. I was so busy editing— Oh dear! What do we do?"

"You put all your papers and that pen in a drawer. And get out of here tout de suite!"

Grams does as she's told without question.

There's a first time for everything.

As she zips past me, she whispers, "What about her?" She points to the crumpled architect on the floor.

"I have an idea. It's probably best if you leave so that you'll have plausible deniability where Silas is concerned."

Ghost-ma's eyes widen, and she snickers as she pops out of the visual plane.

I kneel next to Sophia and ease her strawberry-blonde head from Erick's lap to the floor. "I need you to step back."

He scoots away from the woman and stares inquisitively. "Do I want to know?"

"You do not. Suffice it to say it would be dangerous if you interrupted me. Otherwise, it's as easy as slicing bread."

A scowl darkens his face. "I hope you're not actually going to be slicing anything."

"Figure of speech, Sheriff. Now scoot."

He moves a bit farther away and gives me room to work.

I grasp the woman's petite hand and hold it

firmly in my left. With the pointer finger on my right hand, I carefully trace the reversal symbols that Silas taught me onto her palm.

His words echo in my mind: *Each symbol has many meanings. Connecting them in the precise order is the key to loosening the memory from its resting place. The power of the runes flows through you and takes its form from you. It cannot be undone.*

When he taught me the symbols, he insisted they were highly dangerous if abused or completed incorrectly. Since then, I've had the occasion to use them a handful of times. Practice makes perfect. And my efforts have not been in vain. I complete the series of symbols without interruption, and Erick helps me lift Sophia into a chair.

We wait with bated breath as she slowly regains consciousness.

Ms. Lari blinks rapidly and surveys the room. "Where am I?"

"You're on the third floor of the museum. We were discussing the renovation, and you fainted. Erick caught you and placed you in this chair."

She glances left and right. For a moment she knits her brow, but eventually sighs and retrieves a water bottle from the tote Erick placed beside the chair.

"I must've climbed the stairs too quickly. I

suffer from dangerously low blood pressure. That's why it's so important for me to stay hydrated." She gulps down some water, and I breathe a sigh of relief.

Erick crouches in front of her. "I'm going to run a quick concussion protocol on you. You didn't hit your head. I just want to make sure you're a hundred percent."

She gazes into his dreamy blue eyes and nearly faints again.

He completes the simple "follow my finger with your eyes" portion of the concussion protocol and pronounces her good to go.

We finish the tour, and the fact that she still holds the pieces of my vision for the remodel in her mind is a wonderful indication that I performed the symbols properly. I simply erased her memory of seeing the ghost. Nothing more. Silas will be proud. That is, if I actually tell him.

Erick slips Sophia Lari's arm through the crook of his elbow and helps her down the stairs to the ground floor. If I weren't so happy we'd avoided a paranormal disaster, I'd be hella jealous.

Stepping forward, I shake her hand. "It was wonderful to meet you, Sophia. I look forward to seeing your drawings."

She presses her hand to her left temple and smiles weakly. "Oh, thank you. It was nice to meet you as well. I should have something for you in the next couple of weeks. Unless you're in a rush?"

A little piece of my heart sparkles as I imagine Erick blurting out his proposal plans. No such luck. I fill the silence with a polite reply. "Next couple of weeks will be fine. Thanks again."

Erick releases her arm and pats her hand. "Are you okay to walk to your car, miss?"

Now she blushes. "Thank you, Sheriff. I'll be fine."

As soon as she leaves, I throw on my most mocking tone. "Are you sure you can walk to your car?"

Erick looks offended for a moment. Then he takes in my massive eye roll and chuckles.

Reaching out, I grab his arm and take a shaky breath. "Actually, I'm feeling a little lightheaded. That was two difficult exercises back to back. Can you help me to the apartment?"

He slips an arm around my waist. "Seriously? You're not playing anymore, right?"

My knees wobble, and I grip the fabric of his shirt. "Not at all. I definitely need to lie down. Like, now."

Erick tosses me over his shoulder in a fireman carry, climbs over the chain with ease, and jogs to the apartment.

The severe weakness is the only thing keeping

me from smacking him on the back and squealing my protest. As it is, it's all I can do to keep my eyes open.

He tosses me onto the bed and fetches a glass of water. "Here, drink this. I have to get back to the station. Looks to me like you're about to take a nap, whether or not you want one. Text me when you wake up."

Placing the empty glass on the nightstand, I yawn and flop backward onto the pillows. "Thank you, Prince Charmington."

He softly kisses my cheek and whispers, "You're welcome, Snow Princess."

Before I can protest, I've drifted into a magical dreamland filled with all the accoutrements a snow princess would need, including a handsome prince.

CHAPTER 12

THE ALCHEMICAL WORKINGS from the previous day definitely knocked me out. When I peel my eyelids open, it's morning, and I feel like Rip van Winkle.

Pyewacket lies beside me and must've kept me company all night. Rolling over, I scratch his broad tan head and coo to him adoringly. "Erick's not really your new favorite, is he? I'm your favorite, right, Mr. Cuddlekins? The girl with the opposable thumbs, who fills your bowl with delicious sugary children's cereal. That's your favorite human, right?"

There's a gentle rumbling coming from his throat, but he doesn't offer me the ready sound that I usually take to mean "can confirm." I withdraw my hand and glare at him accusingly. "Robin

Pyewacket Goodfellow, I'm the one who's rushed you to the animal hospital more times than I care to count. And I've been here for you through thick and thin. Don't tell me this reincarnation nonsense has turned you into some kind of fair-weather friend!"

He creeps forward on his belly, and head butts my shoulder.

"All right. I get it, Pye, you're trying to be diplomatic—like a good parent. You love all your humans the same, right?"

"Reow." Can confirm.

"Yeesh." I can't believe he took that seriously. Rolling from the bed, I glance down in confusion. As I clock the sweater and skinny jeans, it takes a few minutes to remember the events of the previous day. Once the information starts flowing, though, it comes back in a powerful rush.

"Yikes! I need to call Silas!"

Pye stretches out one strong paw and thwacks my phone from the nightstand to the floor.

"Rude." As I retrieve the phone, I offer him a warning. "And for that, you're gonna have to wait until I'm done with my phone call, little buddy."

He rolls onto his back and halfheartedly swats in my general direction.

I make it all the way to the settee before flopping down, putting the phone on speaker, and calling my mentor.

"Good morning, Mitzy. It seems a bit early for a call. Shall I assume there is a corpse involved?"

"What is it with everyone jumping to conclusions about me falling over bodies? Oh, and good morning."

He chuckles. "How may I be of assistance?"

"I had an incident yesterday with the architect. She was definitely one of those people who is way too enamored with their own ideas and has significant trouble listening. I sent her an image of what Erick and I envision for the remodel, and it worked amazingly. I thought you'd be pleased."

He harrumphs, and I imagine him smoothing his bushy mustache before he replies. "I must admit, I feel more concern than pleasure. The techniques I share with you are not meant to manipulate the will of those around you."

"No. Never. There aren't many architects in town that work on residential remodels, Silas. She came highly recommended by Amaryllis. I need to work with her and want her to draw up plans for a renovation I actually want. I mean, I'm sure she would make changes and draw up new plans and eventually get where she needs to, but that would waste so much time. Are you mad?"

"Rabid dogs become mad. I find myself disappointed. However, while I agree your intentions were not malicious, alchemy is not meant to serve as a shortcut. You must use it judiciously, and you must never cause harm."

"I understand. But I'm gonna save my apology until I tell you the second thing I did."

A heavy sigh escapes, and I can feel the weight of it through the phone. "I shall keep my concern at bay. I do hope you have done nothing foolish."

Deep breaths. "I want to start things off by saying I had no choice in the matter."

Silas clears his throat loudly. "We always have choices. Perhaps it would be more accurate to state that you didn't take the time to review your options. You made the most convenient choice for reasons you are now using as justification."

Uffda! This guy is definitely not going to let me off the hook. "Fine. But when we got to the third floor of the museum, Grams was up there working on her stories about me. The architect saw the papers and the quill pen moving. She screamed and fainted."

"It appears her weak constitution solved the problem for you. You had plenty of time to concoct a viable story before she awoke."

"Not exactly." Hopefully, he can't hear my strangled swallow.

"Do tell."

"I asked Erick to give me room to work and used the reversal symbols to erase the memory of her seeing Grams—or the memory of seeing the stuff moving of its own accord. I know she didn't actually see Grams, but I didn't want to take any chances."

"My goodness. Perhaps we need to steer your training in the direction of ethics."

"Come on, Silas. Cut me a break. I'm not gonna run my life like Samantha on *Bewitched*. That woman spent more time lying to her husband than she ever spent putting a flip in her hair!"

"I regret I am unfamiliar with the reference. However, if you're saying that using alchemy was the easy way out, once again, I must protest."

He may be right. While I performed the exercise properly and only removed one memory, I had no way of knowing the outcome when I started. Perhaps it would've been better to consider a mundane solution. One that didn't involve potential abuse of power. "I hear what you're saying. You're right. I should've taken more time considering my options. And I think maybe— Maybe a small part of me wanted to show off for Erick."

A soft sigh echoes across the line. "I believe you have uncovered the kernel of your mistake. One must never choose an action based on what others may think. You possess a unique and wonderful set of talents, Mizithra. It would be dangerous to use them carelessly."

"Totally! Makes sense. You're one hundred percent right. I'll definitely slow my roll next time." My cheeks flush with embarrassment. What was I thinking?

"I will assume that is agreement. And I appreciate your honesty in this matter. I have a wonderful book examining ethical principles, Aristotle's *Nicomachean Ethics*. I shall assign it for your next reading. I consider it a fault on my part for not placing the volume in an earlier lesson." There is a moment of silence before he asks, "How goes the investigation?"

"We're waiting on official word from the fire department, but I know it was arson. Kurt is recovering nicely. Although, when I went to the crime scene with him and Artie, he was acting a little bajiggity."

"Ah, you have used that word on a previous occasion. If memory serves, it means having a suspicious nature to his words or behavior. Correct?"

"Yup. Well remembered, Silas."

He laughs openly. "As I'm sure you are aware, Kurt's heritage in the curling scandal of 1975 must weigh heavy on his mind."

"Well, I've heard something about his father being a bad seed. I think Erick might be looking into that. Tapping his connections in the Canadian Mounties to see if there's any record of Marc Frazier entering the country. But this is the first I've heard anything about 1975."

"It may serve you to have a cursory knowledge of the history of this noble sport. It has humble origins, but its proponents are dyed in the wool. You'll be hard-pressed to find anyone without a firm opinion, on one side or the other, with regard to curling."

You don't have to be psychic to see where this is headed. "I would imagine you're just the person to fill me in. Please, enlighten me."

Silas fails to see the humor in my request and proceeds with his TED Talk on the history of curling. "The sport originated on the frozen lochs of Scotland in the sixteenth century. It is rumored the first unofficial competition took place near Paisley Abbey. However, it was not until the 1800s that any formal governing organization existed. Originally known as the Grand Caledonian Curling Club, they were held in such high regard by Queen Victoria that in the 1840s, they were able to gain official endorsement and change their name to the Royal Caledonian Curling Club."

Hopefully, he'll be able to hear my exaggerated yawn on his end of the phone. Whether or not he hears it, the lecture drones on.

"In 1924, the sport had its Olympic debut. At

the time, it was not official, but retroactively it has been acknowledged by all parties concerned. Finally, in the 1950s, they developed a world championship event known as the Scotch Cup. All of these events still ran off the first official set of rules, which held until the International Curling Federation amended them, and, in the late sixties, Air Canada began to sponsor something known as the Silver Broom. Shortly thereafter, in the competition of 1975, the infamous scandal occurred."

I place a hand over my mouth and gasp. "Oh dear, the infamous scandal. I don't see how this possibly has any bearing on my case. But we've come this far. Bowl away."

"The rocks, or stones, are thrown. The only similarity between curling and bowling is perhaps the use of a lane—or, as it's known in the gentlemen's sport, a sheet. The rules that govern which rocks are in play, whether or not a player has made an illegal throw, and who scored a point, are in a league all their own."

"Copy that." I'm still waiting for the part I'm supposed to care about.

"In 1975, there was a highly controversial incident in the final game between the United States and Canada."

If I didn't think Silas would somehow be able to sense my absence through the phone, I'd get up and take a shower. At the rate he's speaking, I may have a solid five to seven minutes before he catches on. Although, there would be hell to pay when he did.

"Are you aware that your grandfather played on the championship team?"

"Yeah, Kurt said something about it. I guess that was the last year they made the trophies out of solid gold, or something like that."

"In fact, it was the only year they made the trophy from solid gold. The entire competition was cloaked in mystery. The order to have the solid gold trophy created came from an anonymous source, along with a hefty donation."

"Sounds like something my Grampa Cal would do."

"Indeed. However, the scandal does not end there. Kurt Frazier's father also played in that championship. He was unmarried at the time and the youngest member of our team. Marc Frazier eventually married Artie, but left soon after their second son was born. Money has always been tight for Artie and her children."

"Ooooh, plot twist. So are you thinking that Kurt took the job at the curling club just to get close to the trophy and that he set the fire to distract from stealing it?"

Silas exhales and patiently waits for me to calm myself. "Perhaps. However, there was a previous attack on the club in the late nineties. The caretaker at the time, Johan Olafsson, foiled the would-be thief and swore it was Marc Frazier."

"I've always liked Johan. Driving his tractor down Main Street to annoy Deputy Paulsen . . . My kinda guy."

Pyewacket emerges from the closet dragging a bag of potato chips in his mouth. He drops it at my feet and stares straight through me.

"Have you suddenly changed your diet, Pye? What's with the chips?"

He continues to glare unblinkingly.

"No argument here, buddy." I grab the bag, tear it open, and shove a handful of crispy chips in my mouth.

Silas harrumphs at my interruption. "As I was saying, it was immediately following that incident that Marc vanished into Canada and was never seen in Pin Cherry again."

"Sounds pretty sus-spish!"

He tactfully ignores my comment. "Artie always claimed that Marc sent her money every month, and a legend grew regarding his seeking employment as an ice-road trucker. Most folks in Pin Cherry were happy to think the best, and the attempted theft was all but forgotten."

"Do you think Kurt is covering for his dad?"

"I have no way of knowing to what lengths a boy might go to protect a myth. I merely wish to provide you with background information. How that information colors your investigation is beyond my control. I simply believe that forewarned is forearmed."

"I appreciate the information. Seems like now might be a good time for me to grab some pastries and attempt to bribe our local law enforcement. They must have some additional information about the origin of the fire."

My mentor offers no input to support my idea. "I wish you safety and success in your sleuthing. Please inform me if I can be of further assistance."

"Thanks. I will."

"And I will drop Aristotle's treatise on ethics at the bookshop the next time I am in town."

"Gee, thanks." I end the call to the sound of my mentor chuckling and stare at my useless mood ring. "I was sort of hoping you'd give me some information on the scandal. For a mood ring that literally came to life in the seventies, you haven't exactly been forthcoming."

The swirls of mysterious grey smoke within the cabochon make no effort to acknowledge my comment.

No message in the ring. No update for the arson wall.

Time to shake things up and get this investigation moving.

Abandoning the chips on the coffee table, I proceed to the next order of business. Now, what does one wear to a bribing?

CHAPTER 13

PARKING DIRECTLY in front of Rex's Drugstore, I walk the half block back to the station with my pink box of treats in hand. My red holiday sweater, with its plunging, crisscross neckline, is the perfect complement to the pastries.

This time, I walk straight into the sheriff's office. If I want my best chance, I need to give him the pick of the litter.

"Good morning, Sheriff Harper. Can I interest you in a cheese Danish?"

Opening the cardboard lid as though it's the polished golden cover on an ancient treasure chest, I lean forward and waft the scent of pastries toward my boyfriend.

Erick looks up and runs a hand across his furrowed brow. He grins like a schoolboy when he catches sight of the backdrop to my offering and avoids my gaze. "Maybe a sugar rush would do me some good. This case is going nowhere fast, Moon."

That sounds like an invitation to me. I drop my caboose in the visitor's chair and stare with rapt attention. "Nothing helpful from the arson investigator?"

"Not terribly. They've traced the point of origin of the fire to the lounge in the curling club. There are people in and out of there all day. Technically, there's no smoking allowed indoors, but I've personally been on-site when someone has bent the rules. So the presence of an ashtray, on what was once a side table, isn't terribly incriminating. Plus, if the cigarette was in the ashtray, there's virtually no way it would've set the sofa on fire. Which seems to be the only thing flammable in the vicinity of the fire's theoretical point of origin."

"That is a puzzler, Sheriff."

For the first time since I arrived, he makes eye contact. A genuine smile spreads across his face like warm butter on a stack of pancakes. "You caught me off guard, Moon. But now that I've had the chance to drink in your facial expression and the 'full package,' I'd say you're up to no good. Let's cut to the chase."

"Touché. I think Kurt is hiding something. I'm

not all the way to believing he's to blame, but maybe he's covering for Marc?"

"I know what you mean. His story mostly checks out, but something about the delivery of it didn't sit right with me, either. I asked Kurt to stop by the medical examiner's office so she could get a better look at his head injury. I had to tell him a little fib."

I widen my eyes and gasp. "Sheriff Harper! I'm flabbergasted."

He laughs and takes a huge bite of cheese Danish, chews, and swallows hastily. "I don't mean this in a chauvinistic way, but would you mind grabbing me a coffee?"

Jumping from the chair, I collect the box of pastries and head to the break room.

Deputy Johnson is draining the last drips of coffee from the pot into a paper cup.

"Tell you what, Johnson, you give me that cup of coffee for the sheriff, and I'll give you this entire box of pastries."

His eyes light up like a kid at Christmas. "Deal!" He hands me the sludgy, slightly burnt bottom-of-the-pot cup of coffee, and I hand him eleven of the patisserie's best options. "Thanks, Deputy."

Johnson takes the box with two hands and inhales deeply. "Thank you!"

When I get back to Erick's office, he's licking

flaky pastry off his fingertips. He reaches for the cup of coffee and slugs half of it down the hatch without blinking.

After the initial shock, I have to comment. "It's amazing what a couple of tours in Afghanistan and several years in law enforcement can do to your taste buds."

He winks. "Oh, the coffee is disgusting, but beggars can't be choosy."

Returning to the uncomfortable wooden chair, I nod encouragingly. "So you were confessing your sins of prevarication."

He tilts his head and arches an eyebrow. "Silas?"

"Yep, he's better than one of those word-a-day calendars."

We share a chuckle. He finishes the rest of his blackened coffee and continues his story about Kurt. "Anyway, I told him we needed to get an impression of the wound so that we could match a weapon to it. And, also, that could help us find the arsonist. In actuality, I asked the medical examiner to take a look at the angle of the wound and determine if it was self-inflicted." He leans back and crosses his arms.

My head nods fervently. "This is what I'm saying. I'm so glad we're on the same wavelength. You'll let me know what you find out, right?"

"That feels like a rhetorical question."

I shrug and attempt an innocent smile. "Is the curling club lounge on the second floor?"

He shakes his head slowly. "Not entirely. It has two levels. Second floor has floor-to-ceiling windows for viewing the games. Ground floor is more for hanging out and snacking. Point of origin was on the ground floor. Plus, the investigator said, with a building that old, it doesn't take much to send it up like a tinderbox. All wooden construction, wood paneling on the interior, and nothing treated with fire retardant. Honestly, he was surprised the fire didn't spread faster."

"Maybe it would have if Artie hadn't called the paramedics so fast."

"What's that now?" Erick leans forward eagerly.

"Artie said she was on the phone with Kurt when he was attacked. She heard him groan and then a crash, which she assumed was the phone hitting the floor. She called the paramedics immediately, and I guess the fire trucks followed. So, when Amaryllis and I arrived, they didn't seem at all surprised to hear there was someone trapped inside. They just had no idea where to look."

Erick nods. "But you cleared that up for them, right?"

"Correction, the tipster that I happened to be on the phone with cleared it up."

Erick's blue eyes twinkle. "And by tipster, you mean the voices in your head?"

"You're not wrong."

As I'm ready to launch into the next phase of my bribery, the cracked plastic phone on Erick's desk rings incessantly.

He grabs it without looking. "Sheriff Harper." His pose is casual, and his tone confident.

Remind me never to play poker with this man. Despite my powerful extrasensory perceptions, I can't get a clear read.

"Understood. You too."

"What's up?"

He hangs up the receiver and shuffles some papers on his desk.

"Well? How long do you plan on keeping me in suspense?" With the pastry box traded for the last cup of coffee in the station, I cross my arms and let my flirty festive sweater do its work.

Erick attempts to resist my efforts, but the hint of pink on his cheeks and a detectable increase in his heart rate sell him out.

"I'm waiting, Sheriff."

He lets out an exasperated sigh and shakes his head. "I was planning on telling you, Moon. Don't think your feminine wiles turned the table. I only wanted to see how long I could resist your mind probe."

"Mind probe! I don't like the sound of that one bit. I'm not some alien overlord, Sheriff."

Erick nods but also shrugs. "I know exactly what you're made of Miss Moon. I only want to make sure we keep the playing field as level as possible."

"Whatever you have to tell yourself." I make no effort to disguise my frown of disagreement. "Now, spill."

"That was the medical examiner. Whatever was used to induce Kurt's unconsciousness left no definable imprint. Technically, that's good. If they'd hit him with enough force to leave a distinct impression in his occipital bone, he may never have awakened. However, that sends us right back to square one. The items in the storage closet all had Kurt's prints. Which, of course, makes perfect sense. Either the attacker brought his own weapon and left with it, or Kurt knocked himself out."

"Rather than being technical, sheriff, let's be possible. Maybe Kurt was never actually unconscious. Some time did elapse between the phone call with his mother and my arrival on scene. Did the firemen mention if he was conscious when they found him?"

"He was conscious and banging on the locked door."

Tilting my head from side to side, I process this information. "Either he regained consciousness before they rescued him, or he never hit himself hard enough to lose it, to begin with."

Erick leans back, and the springs in his vintage chair screech with protest. He laces his fingers behind his head and chews the inside of his cheek.

My nonexistent patience takes over. "What are you thinking? Maybe we should—"

He rockets forward, allowing his arms to thud onto the desk. "Give me a second to catch up. Yes, we should bring Kurt in for further questioning."

Smiling brightly, I edge forward and lift one finger. Before I can slather on my so-called charm, Deputy Paulsen waddles to the doorway and loudly clears her throat.

I offer a neutral greeting. "Hey, Paulsen."

She glances at me and sucks a bit of air in between her teeth. It's unclear whether the sound is meant to be dismissive or patronizing. Honestly, it's a little of both.

"How can I help you, Deputy?" Erick gives his full attention to Paulsen.

"I thought we oughta question Johan Olafsson. He always swore it was Marc Frazier that tried to steal the trophy all those years ago, and he was practically the skip during the '75 ship. He'd know if the beef on the sheet still carries any weight."

Some of what she's saying makes sense, but most of the jargon goes right over my head.

"I like the idea, Paulsen, but we both know Olafsson is no fan of yours. I'll head out there and see what I can find. I've heard eight or ten versions of what went down at that championship game in 1975. If anyone can give me a first-hand of what happened on the sheet that day, it would be former team captain and then coach Olafsson. Thanks for the lead."

"You betcha, Sheriff." Paulsen frowns and shrugs in my general direction. Definitely dismissive. She spins on her heel, and the swish-swish of polyester fibers rubbing heralds her exit.

No time like the present to tout my friendly terms with Johan. "Hey, you know, I'm on—"

Erick puts up a hand and shakes his head. "You're welcome to come along to the Olafsson place. I know what you and Silas did for him and his wife. I'm sure he'd be happy to see you."

What Silas and I did for Johan Olafsson and his wife was some time before the sheriff and I were any kind of official couple. I secretly hoped Erick hadn't heard about my rule-bending. Clearly, this local lawman always has one ear to the ground.

"Sounds good. I look forward to catching up with the Olafssons."

The sheriff grabs his jacket and the keys to his cruiser. He slips an arm around my waist as we head out the door and whispers in my ear. "I'd ask you to let me do the talking, but I think I've made enough futile requests for one day."

"Copy that, Sheriff."

CHAPTER 14

ON THE DRIVE out to the Olafsson farmstead, Erick
seems lost in thought. Although, I could be project-
ing. Johan and his wife Marguerite have been
through hell. She was diagnosed with a rare form of
brain cancer, and their insurance didn't cover the
necessary specialized treatments. I stumbled across
their situation quite by accident, and Silas was only
too happy to facilitate a rescue mission via the Duncan-Moon Foundation. At first, Johan sent frequent
updates, but I'm sure the emotionally draining role
of staying positive to support his wife took its toll.
Last I heard, he'd committed to Alcoholics Anonymous, and it's been months since I saw his tractor
plodding down Main Street.

Glancing down at my antique mood ring, I long
for a flash of good news. The swirls of dark smoke

inside the cabochon shift to deep blue as we turn down the drive. The color brings back an instant memory of Marguerite ravaged by her illness. I place my right hand over the ring and blink back tears. Hopefully, the old tractor parked next to his pickup truck is a good sign.

When the car stops, I hop out before Erick has time to turn off the engine.

Mounting the two cement steps, I knock on the front door, step back, and wait. A smiling woman with the flirty blonde curls of Meg Ryan in *French Kiss* opens the front door and beams in my general direction. Probably a care nurse.

I grin in return, but it never touches my eyes. "Good afternoon. I was hoping to speak to Mr. Olafsson. Do you know if he's home?"

The woman's smile splits into a huge "aw shucks" grin, and she offers me her hand. "Mitzy Moon! If it isn't the Lord's little angel come to visit. Come in! Come in!"

I hesitate on the cold stone step and stare in shock. "Marguerite?" The last time I saw this woman, she appeared to be death warmed over. Sunken eyes, dark circles, and a haphazard turban wrapped around her frail skull.

She turns. "As I live and breathe. If you came to check on your investment, I can assure you it's paid off in spades. Have a seat in the parlor, and I'll put the kettle on. Coffee or hot chocolate?"

Speechless, I stumble into the front room, which smells of fresh-baked cookies, and thankfully Erick replies for the both of us. "We'll have a couple of cocoas, Marguerite. You're looking fantastic. Are you feeling well?"

She hollers up the stairs for Johan and calls out from the kitchen above the clanging of pots and pans. "I haven't felt this good since I was forty-five, Sheriff. The doctors don't know what to make of it. They sure weren't in my corner when this whole thing started."

Erick senses the emotion lurking behind my faceplate and slides a comforting arm around my shoulders.

Johan clomps down the stairs, catches sight of the sheriff, and places both hands in the air as he walks into the living room. "I swear, Sheriff, I've been keeping my nose clean. Haven't touched a drop of alcohol in seventeen months. As God and Marguerite are my witnesses."

The sheriff hops to his feet, shakes Johan's hand, and pats him on the shoulder. "I've heard nothing but good things since you got on the straight and narrow, Mr. Olafsson. Mitzy and I only stopped by to pick your brain about the old curling team. Can you spare a few minutes?"

The aging man peeks around the sheriff and seems to see me for the first time. Huge wet tears spring to the corners of his eyes, and he lunges forward to wrap me in a bear hug. "I have all the time in the world for Miss Moon. Pardon my inappropriate greeting, miss, but around here, your name is as sacred as fishing, curling, and lutefisk."

I'm not sure whether to be offended or flattered. "Thank you, Mr. Olafsson. It's wonderful to see Marguerite looking so healthy."

He slaps his knee and takes a seat in his recliner. "You betcha. Not a day goes by I'm not grateful that things turned around—for both of us." Johan rummages in the pocket of his dungarees and pulls out his AA chip, passing it to me as though it's the Holy Grail. I take it with reverence.

"You know, my grandmother was a big believer. She was over fifteen years sober when she passed." I hand the chip back. He accepts it and slides it into his pocket as he nods solemnly. "That's one record I hope to beat."

This time my smile crinkles the corners of my eyes as I nod enthusiastically. "I think you and Marguerite are off to a great start."

She enters carrying a tray filled with mugs, a plate of holiday cookies, and a can of whipped cream.

Johan jumps up from the recliner, relieves her

of the tray, and shoos her toward the sofa. "Sit down. Sit down. No need to show off." He passes out the mugs of cocoa, offers whipped cream—of which I'm the only taker—and finally passes the plate of cookies.

Once the refreshments are out of the way, Erick gets down to business. "At the time of the 1975 championship game, you transitioned from team captain to coach. Is that right?"

"That's correct, sheriff. Cal Duncan was a heckuva thrower. And he also tossed money around like nobody's business. We needed him to help us beat the Canadians, and I knew a spot as team captain would lock him in."

Erick nods. "And Marc Frazier? How long had he been on the team at that point?"

"It was only his second season, but he was a natural. Nobody could move the broom like that kid. His throws were inconsistent, but his broom work—boy, I can see it like it was yesterday."

"I'll bet. I heard a lot of stories about what happened that day, Mr. Olafsson. I'd love to hear the truth."

Johan swallows the last bite of his frosted Christmas cookie, sets his mug of hot cocoa on the side table, and leans back in his recliner. "Cal's toss was perfection. The gods themselves couldn't have thrown a more perfect stone. The release was clean, and we were headed toward a raised double takeout to steal three and take the ship. When the rock stopped, we celebrated." He pauses and closes his eyes. His face transforms as he relives the vivid memory. "I saw Marc's foot touch the rock."

The sheriff places a hand on his gut and groans as though someone has punched him in the breadbasket. "That must've hurt."

Johan exhales long and slow. "It should have. Curling is a gentleman's sport. No referees to watch the stones. Each man is meant to make an honest reckoning of his actions. Marc claimed the Canadians were lying about the burnt rock, and Cal backed him all the way to the podium." He hangs his head and rubs a gnarled hand over his face. "Never felt right about it, but I kept my mouth shut. I thought there was honor in supporting my team. Looking back, who knows? Marc was a bad seed. He had been using the team's travel to shuffle pills back and forth across the border. And then in the nineties, when he tried to steal the trophy— Well, I wish I woulda spoke up. That's all I'm gonna say."

Erick lets the moment of silence hang. He sips his cocoa and finishes another cookie. "Mr. Olafsson, what makes you so sure it was Marc who tried to steal the trophy?"

Johan's face turns hard. "I looked him right in his little weasel face. Those beady, deceitful eyes. I cracked him upside the head with a hockey stick, and he took off with his tail between his legs. I never saw him again. But this latest hoopla at the arena makes me wonder if Kurt is following in his father's footsteps. Did you search the kid's place?"

Erick shakes his head and wipes hot chocolate from the corner of his mouth. "We need to find Marc Frazier. I'm going to get in touch with a buddy of mine who works for the Mounties. If we can rule out any involvement by the elder Frazier, then we'll have to take a more serious look at Kurt. He never struck me as the type, but I suppose I could be wrong about this one."

Johan shakes his head in commiseration. "I know what you mean, Sheriff. I never saw a kid work harder. He came in every day after school and groomed the sheets, organized the equipment, re-stocked the vending machines, and polished the trophies. I never had to worry about them once. By the time he graduated high school, he had keys to the whole place—even the trophy case with the solid gold stone. Tell you what, I never lost a wink of sleep thinking about it."

Marguerite passes the plate of cookies around once again. "I just wanted you to know, Miss Moon. I'm in remission. My doctors are quite hopeful. Can't thank you enough for what you did for our family."

I gaze at the floor and mumble some humble gratitude.

Johan adds a bit of whipped cream to his hot chocolate. "They say there's a big storm coming. That'll put a nice layer up in the hills. Come run off, the fields should be more than ready for an early planting. I think this will be my best crop of corn yet."

Erick gazes at me over the rim of his mug and lifts an eyebrow. I attempt a nonchalant nod.

The missus leans forward and hands me the plate of frosted cookies one more time. Whether it's obligation or obsession, it takes very little to convince me to have another. "Thank you. These cookies are amazing, Marguerite."

"Well, thanks. That's my grandmother's recipe. She always said it was the almond extract that made the difference. Glad you like them."

Now the master of the house sets his mug down and sighs. "Sure am glad I rotated the crops last year. Be a real shame to waste the season on alfalfa, especially when I can get myself a bumper crop of corn. Who knows, we may even find the time to set up a corn maze for the kids."

Now I'm looking at Erick and arching my eyebrow. He inhales and slaps his right hand on his knee. "Welp . . ."

I glance around the room and find myself the

only one without a decoder ring. Marguerite grabs
the tray and scurries off to the kitchen, and Johan
gets to his feet. "S'pose you better get back to the
station, Sheriff. I know Pin Cherry can't get along
without you for long. Sure appreciate the visit. You
let me know when you find that weasel, Marc Frazier. I got a bone to pick with that fella."

Erick calls into the kitchen. "Thank you for the
hospitality, Mrs. Olafsson."

Jumping on the quickly departing train, I add,
"Yes, thank you, Marguerite."

We grab our coats and step out the front door.

Johan and Marguerite follow us, and as we
climb into the cruiser, they walk down the front
steps, still waving.

Erick backs up the vehicle, and I inhale in
preparation for my question.

"Hold on a minute longer, Mitzy," he mumbles
like a professional ventriloquist.

We head down the drive as Johan and Marguerite walk behind, waving as we depart. When
they finally disappear into the fields of snow in the
rearview, Erick exhales. "Okay, you're clear to
speak, Moon."

"What in the heck did I just witness?"

"That's what anthropologists call social mores
in Birch County."

His unexpectedly affected scholarly response

tickles my funny bone, and I laugh until I have to catch my breath. "So, that was considered etiquette?"

He grins. "You betcha. It's always better for the host or hostess to remind you that you have other duties to attend to. It's considered rude to think so highly of yourself that you announce it on your own."

"Wow. I think I finally know how Jane Goodall felt."

CHAPTER 15

SEEING THE OLAFSSONS SO HAPPY—IN such a different place in their lives—hits me with a wave of nostalgia for my recent past in almost-Canada.

Erick is busy talking to dispatch on the radio, and it's a testament to the depth of the emotion I'm feeling that I'm not paying any attention. My gaze is out the window and across the bleak winter fields, and my mind is somewhere else entirely. Whether I overhear something or the idea comes as a psychic message, it's difficult to be sure. "Hey, can you drop me at my dad's before you reach out to CC?"

The sheriff runs a hand through his slicked-back blond hair and nods. "I'm a little surprised you don't want to eavesdrop on that call. Are you feeling okay?"

"Yeah. That visit got me thinking about my life

here. It's been a little over three years, and it seems like the blink of an eye some days. Definitely feels like my dad and I need to do something about my grandpa Cal's legacy."

Erick tilts his head and bobs it in a decidedly Robert De Niro fashion. "You wouldn't be trying to rewrite history, would you?"

"What do you mean?" Genuine innocence floods my features.

He taps his thumb on the steering wheel for a moment before responding. "I have no reason to question Mr. Olafsson's version of events. If your grandfather knowingly covered up the burnt stone and accepted a championship his team didn't deserve—"

"Oh, I totally believe what Johann said. And what's a burnt stone?" My mouth curls up in confusion.

Long-suffering boyfriend, Erick Harper, chuckles. "If a player touches a curling stone after it crosses the blue line—no matter how slightly—it is out of play, and no points can be taken."

"Yeesh! Those are harsh rules. But the more I find out about my grandfather's past deeds, the more I have to shake my head."

Erick exhales and mumbles in agreement.

"What I'd like to talk to my dad about is coming up with some way to make up for what my grandfather did. We need to make it up to the community but also to the Canadian team. My dad's a sports guy. He'll know what to do."

There's an unexpected edge to Erick's reply. "I'm a sports guy."

It's unlike him to be defensive. "Hey, I wasn't trying to pull your man card or anything. I just need to talk to my dad, all right?"

His shoulders relax, and he bobs his square jaw as he makes the turn onto First Avenue. Hopping out of the cruiser, I run across the street, shockingly staying on my feet, and wave to Erick as he pulls toward Main Street and the sheriff's station.

The snow covering the ground adds an eerie hush to the world. Like the moment before the voiceover recording queue in a sound booth, the silence is deafening.

Hurrying past the historical marker with its large bronze plaque commemorating the original Iron Range Brewing Company, I rush into the warm interior of the Duncan Restorative Justice Foundation and take a moment to appraise the life-size bronze statue of Cal Duncan.

While I feel dwarfed by the impressive vaulted ceilings and ornamental plaster cornices, my grandfather towers defiantly above the terrazzo floor. Master of all he surveys. If anyone could've benefitted from the *Spiderman* "with great power comes great responsibility" speech, it would've been this guy.

There's a new receptionist at the lobby desk, yet, just like her predecessors, she seems to instantly know who I am. It might have something to do with the fact that my father and I share the same shockingly white hair and mysterious grey eyes. Although, I've always suspected there's a photo of me taped near the phone. She smiles and waves me toward the elevator.

When the bell pings at the penthouse level, my barrel-chested father is waiting with a concerned look on his face. "I'm pretty sure I know why you're here."

"You heard about the arena?"

"Oh, I thought you were here about the '75 scandal."

"You're not wrong. Turns out there might be more than a passing connection."

After a proper father-daughter hug and updates on the shopping trip that currently occupies my stepmother and stepbrother, we retire to my father's study to discuss the arson and the scandal.

"I grew up bragging about my dad tossing the winning rock. More than once, I had to justify the authenticity of that championship. Cal always told the same story when I asked him about it, but something never sat right with me. Based on all the bad choices Marc Frazier made, you'd have to assume it never sat well with him either."

"Do you think he wanted to tell the truth, and Grandpa Cal convinced him to keep his mouth shut?" Concern tightens my jaw.

"Oh, never." Jacob bats the suggestion away with a wave of his large hand. "It takes a felon to recognize one, remember?"

His open reference to his criminal past catches me off guard. He's come such a long way toward putting things right and paying it forward; some days, I forget he ever did hard time for his part in a big box store robbery almost twenty years ago. The thing I love about my father is that *he* never forgets. He wakes up every day determined to make better decisions and leave the world a better place than he found.

"I'm glad you started this foundation, Dad. I've learned a lot about giving back since I came to Pin Cherry Harbor. Offering ex-cons a solid chance at rehabilitation—10 out of 10." I give him a thumbs up. "Would recommend."

He puts an arm around my shoulders and gives me a playful squeeze. "Who would've thought? A couple of hoodlums like us, each turning over new *leafs* and everything."

We share a laugh, and I turn the discussion back to making amends. "Erick is going to use his contact in the Canadian Mounties to track down Marc Frazier. Although I'm not prepared to put any eggs in a basket so already full of rotten ones—maybe Marc will confess to what he did, and maybe he won't. Meantime, I was thinking you and I should join forces, or our foundations should join forces, and rebuild the ice arena. Hockey, figure skating, and curling are so important to the community. I'd like to get it rebuilt as quickly as possible."

He smiles warmly. "If it wasn't for that hair, I'd wonder if I actually made a daughter so amazing. You really are special, Mitzy, and not just because of your powers."

"Thanks, Dad." The years of life without him hurt a little less each day. "So, what do you think?"

Jacob rubs his chin thoughtfully. "I always heard it put this way: you can do things fast, good, or cheap. Pick two. If you want to build a proper ice arena and you want it done quickly, it's going to take money. Lucky for the town, you and I have an abundance."

"It's so funny that you would say that about fast, good, or cheap. Believe it or not, it's one of the first things they taught me in film school. People work on these different student films, and they always think they're gonna emulate the big studio productions. And, of course, with modern technology, you've got a decent shot. If you have enough *time* and *money*. The problem with student films—they're always on a tight to nonexistent budget and always racing toward the deadline!"

He sniffs sharply and nods. "I'm so sorry I didn't know about your mother passing away. I wish I'd been around to make a difference in your life. Maybe you would've stayed in school."

His after-school special comment brings a snort from my snarky nose. "You can't be serious? First of all, Grams and I have played this game many times, and we always end up at the same place. Everything happens for a reason. All the choices and events in our lives lead us to where we are. I'm super happy where I am. So, ipso facto or ergo blah blah Latin, I wouldn't change anything. Plus, weren't you in the middle of a rather extended stay in the state penitentiary at that point in my life?"

He breaks eye contact and shakes his head. "Yeah. I suppose I wouldn't have been winning any father of the year awards even if I had tried to be part of your life."

I squeeze his powerful arm and wink. "Not to worry, Jacob Duncan, you're the father of the year every year now. I honestly couldn't be happier to have you in my life. Thank you for working so hard to make up for lost time."

He leans forward and hugs me firmly. "Thank you for letting me."

Fortunately, my father offers to take care of the logistical side of the arena building. He's gained a lot of experience in business after running my grandfather's railroad empire and has plenty of contacts in the commercial architecture and construction industries.

"I'll take care of the announcement. I'm sure Quince Knudsen is home for the holidays, and you and I both know nobody takes a picture like that kid!"

My father agrees and walks me to the elevator.

Outside the Restorative Justice Foundation, another wave of nostalgia sweeps over me. I wander down to Main Street and into the cul-de-sac beside my bookshop.

The pristine blanket of snow covering the great lake brings visions of the mysterious Snow Princess to my head. Shaking it off, I turn and gaze up our partially abandoned Main Street. Something about the beautiful holiday bunting and the warm glow of the streetlights in the gloaming shifts the vision toward one of magic and promise.

It reminds me of the way my vision shifted when I placed that first foot on the sidewalk in Pin Cherry Harbor. The smelly bus pulled away, and I gazed across the narrow street to be welcomed by the neon sign of Myrtle's Diner.

I had no way of knowing how influential that

simple eating establishment would become in my life. It's where I first met the adorably proper Sheriff Erick Harper. It's where I ran for reassurance after my first terrible tornado. And it's where I learned to trust some of the most important people in my life. Silas. Odell. Jacob. And, of course, Erick. It may sound strange to say that life is like a plate of french fries, but, in my opinion, french fries are the single most glorious substance on the planet. And a life well lived— Well, it's the same.

A biting wind kicks up, and a swirl of snow envelops me in frosty reality. I head inside the bookshop and stop short as I come face-to-face with the architect.

"Mitzy! I was hoping to find you here."

"It's where I live." Snark level five out of ten. I must've left the bookshop unlocked. That's not something I would normally do, but I suppose this curling case has me distracted.

Sophia gestures toward the printing museum. "May we go inside and spread out the plans? I'd love to show you how things are coming along. I think you'll be really pleased."

Grams shimmers into existence just above Sophia's head. "Play nice, Mitzy. She's weeks ahead of schedule. Clearly, the woman's excited about the project."

I exhale my resistance. "Follow me."

Leading the way into the printing museum, I flip on the lights and offer the surface of a display case filled with vintage movable type as a place to spread out her plans.

She unrolls the blueprints, sets up her laptop, and gestures for me to stand beside her. "I brought the blueprints in case your boyfriend was here, but if you're like me, you'd rather see the 3D modeling. I know you're going to love the finishes I've chosen."

At the mention of my boyfriend and finishes, I wonder if I should fire off a text.

Too late.

Sophia launches an application and steps back. A virtual tour of my soon-to-be home begins—complete with an upbeat soundtrack. The good news is that she's modeled all the spaces exactly as I envisioned. The bad news? And believe me, there is bad news! She's gone ultramodern with the finishes. Not at all what Erick and I discussed.

I'm tempted to toss another psychic vision her way, but Silas and his ethics have not been lost on me. "The layout is fantastic. Can you leave the plans with me? I'd love to go over them with Sheriff Harper, but he's in the middle of a big case. It may take us a few days to give them the proper attention."

She momentarily frowns but quickly recovers. "I don't have any way to leave the virtual walk-through. It's a massive file. It's not like I can email it or anything."

More flies with honey, Grams always says. "Why don't we take it one step at a time? We'll go over the blueprints and make sure we're all on the same page with the construction. Then we'll have plenty of time to discuss finishes during the demo phase. Right?"

She grins nervously. "Of course. Let me know when you and . . . Is it Erick?"

I nod and smile. My mama raised me right.

"Let me know when you and Erick have some time for me, and I'll stop over to show him the virtual tour."

Using my newfound Birch County etiquette, I gently place a hand on her arm and steer her toward an exit. "That sounds wonderful. I'm sure with your skills, you have plenty of clients to juggle. Don't let me keep you."

She flushes at the unexpected compliment, and before she can recover, I have her out the door and on her way.

After a quick text to Erick, I can officially kick my feet up for the day.

CHAPTER 16

JUST AS MY lazy eyelids are about to surrender, my inconsiderate cell phone pings with a text notification. Halfheartedly sweeping the coffee table with my left hand, I search for the offending device and gaze down through the nearly drawn curtain of my eyelids.

"Station. Now. You're not gonna believe it."

I'd like to say the blunt, demanding text offends. Not a chance. Erick hit all the right notes. My eyes are wide open, and my over-clocked curiosity chip is whirring out of control.

Shoving my feet into winter boots, I zip my coat as I hurry down the circular staircase.

It doesn't take a psychic to predict this future.

My distraction with outerwear causes a biomechanical miscalculation. The trailing foot catches on the "No Admittance" chain, and I tumble roots over shoots into the stacks.

Thankfully, my resident ghost is otherwise occupied, and the last I saw my fiendish fur baby, he was sprawled across my antique bed.

Dusting myself off, I make a quick check of my extremities to make sure all is well as I dash through the side door and walk briskly toward the station.

As soon as I darken the doorway, Deputy Gilbert, who's filling in at the front desk, jerks his thumb toward the back. "Sheriff said you left your purse in the observation room. Head on back."

My purse? Hilarious. Although, it says something about the lack of observation in our younger deputies that this Gilbert fellow never noticed my lack of purse-iness.

Rather than argue the finer points of wardrobe accessories, which I may or may not carry, I push through the crooked wooden gate, hustle across the vacant bullpen, and duck into the observation room.

A jolt of shock freezes me in my tracks.

The room is not empty. Deputies Paulsen and Johnson have pulled up chairs and are opening bags of snacks.

Paulsen nods. "Have a seat, Moon. You're not gonna want to miss this."

Finally, gathering my wits about me, I turn and look through the one-way glass into the interrogation room. Erick is seated across the table from Kurt Frazier and seems to be informing him of his rights for the second or third time.

I grab a chair and accept the bag of barbecue chips Johnson hands me.

"Kurt, are you absolutely sure you don't want a lawyer present?"

If I didn't know better, I'd think Erick was attempting to advise the criminal against making a statement.

Kurt shakes his head vigorously. "No. I'm serious, Sheriff Harper. I can't take the guilt anymore. I came in to confess—clear my conscience. Is that thing recording?" Kurt gestures to the device on the table, and Erick answers verbally, for the record. "We are recording this confession, Mr. Frazier. Please begin when you're ready."

Sheriff Harper leans back and crosses his arms. The vibe rolling off his shoulders is not one of triumph over a crime solved. He's upset by Kurt's rash decision.

I can see where he's coming from. We're still waiting on the information about Marc Frazier, and we've by no means exhausted all of our leads. Sure, there were parts of Kurt's story that didn't quite jive, but even my extra senses didn't peg him as an arsonist.

Kurt makes a fist with his left hand and nervously rubs his knuckles with the right. He doesn't make eye contact with Sheriff Harper. He stares at the table and seems to repeat a prepared speech.

"I took a lot of teasing about the '75 ship."

Erick does not lean forward but seeks to clarify. "Mr. Frazier, are you referring to the 1975 World Curling Championship?"

"Yeah. The '75 ship. People still talk about that game and whether or not my dad burnt that stone. I defended him every time it came up. I wanted to believe my dad was a good guy."

The sheriff nods.

Kurt pauses, and I can almost hear his teeth grind as the muscles in his jaw flex. "I did believe it— Until . . ." He exhales painfully. "When he tried to steal the trophy in '98, I was furious. All the times I took a punch in the schoolyard— Never mind. Point is, I wanted to put an end to it. I needed to make that trophy disappear forever. So, I figured the best way to make it happen would be to burn the whole place down. Leave no evidence for anyone. So I set the fire, locked myself in the storage room, and pretended to knock myself out."

For a man who claims to be confessing to clear his conscience, Kurt does not look relieved. His shoulders are still knitted together with tension, and he refuses to look up from the table.

Erick straightens in his chair and inhales. "Mr. Frazier, how did you start the fire?"

Kurt briefly throws both of his hands in the air before re-gripping his left fist with the right hand. "What does it matter? I did it. Okay? Just charge me with the arson or whatever, and case closed."

My fair-minded lawman rolls his shoulders back, and I sense a growing frustration. "That's not how it works, Kurt. We don't tie a neat bow on the case with a ribbon made of lies. You need to verify this information, and if your explanation is consistent with the evidence, then I will accept your confession. But if you're confessing to protect someone, I suggest you tell me the truth immediately."

Paulsen mumbles her agreement next to me.

Kurt swallows hard but says nothing.

Sheriff Harper presses on. "Next question. What did you use to knock yourself out?"

"I hit myself with a hockey stick."

Erick makes a note on his pad. The gesture seems more for show than anything else. The confession is being recorded. If he needs any information, he can easily go back and replay that part.

"Fine. And where is the trophy?"

This question brings a wave of fear from Kurt. He fidgets in his seat and draws a ragged breath. "I took it out to my ice house and chucked it through the spearfishing hole."

Angling forward, I quiet my internal mono-logue and evaluate Kurt's last statement. It feels different from anything else he said. And that flash of fear . . .

Paulsen pipes up next to me. "That's the only honest thing he said in this whole farce of a confession."

Maybe I'm not the only psychic in the room. Turning toward her, I nod in agreement. "True, but there's more. Something he said doesn't check out."

For a split second, her face reflects the relaxed woman I joined on a rescue adventure in the canoeing country far north of Pin Cherry. Her right hand is deep in a bag of cheese puffs and nowhere near her gun. She nods in cursory agreement. "I know what you mean, Moon. It's true, but not quite true."

Johnson leans toward me and offers a surreptitious look of shock. Clearly, he's aware of how rare it is for Deputy Pauly Paulsen to agree with anyone other than herself.

Turns out we're not the only ones with questions. My smart, sexy boyfriend is clearly on Team Doubt.

"Mr. Frazier, I spoke to your mother in the diner last week. She said the old Frazier icehouse got left on the lake too long last year and went down with about seven others during the early thaw. When did you get a new icehouse?"

Silence thickens the air, and Kurt's chin slowly lifts. His golden-brown eyes are filled with terror. He looks directly at the sheriff and states in no uncertain terms. "I stole the trophy. I threw it into the lake. I set the fire at the arena, and I knocked myself out. I'm the one you want. I did it all."

Erick stops the recording, gets to his feet, and turns toward the observation room. "Deputies, let's get that confession transcribed and let Mr. Frazier sign his John Hancock to it. Then we'll place him under arrest and process him."

He places a hand on the table and leans toward Kurt. "I don't know what you're scared of, but I know you didn't do this, Kurt. At least not all of it."

That last phrase would indicate that Erick believes some part—possibly the bit about the trophy. No time to waste. I slip out of the observation room and grab a seat in his office.

He walks in, sees me, hangs his head, and closes the door. "Well? Anything?"

As he trudges toward his chair, I share what I know. "He's genuinely terrified of something—or someone. But he absolutely did not set the fire. He absolutely did not knock himself out. However, something happened between him and that trophy. That's worth looking into."

Erick scrunches up his face in confusion. "How? Are you suggesting we bring in a Coast Guard cutter to break up the ice and dredge the lake to find some long-lost golden trophy?"

Ouch! I know he's frustrated, and while it's not directly aimed at me, his words hurt. "Hey, I'm on—"

The phone on his desk rings loudly. He grabs the receiver. "Sheriff Harper."

His jaw clenches. "Whoa. Whoa. Whoa. Hold on, CC. Mitzy is in my office. I'm putting you on speaker." He messes with a few buttons, and eventually, the sexy, French-Canadian voice of my favorite Mountie fills the room. "*Bonjour, Mademoiselle* Moon."

Erick rolls his eyes and chuckles. "Dial it down a notch, buddy. How many times have I gotta tell you, she's spoken for?"

"As am I, *Monsieur*. However, one must appreciate beauty whenever one can."

Leaning toward the speaker, I attempt to back up Erick. "I appreciate the compliment, CC. Let's stick to business. Did you find Marc Frazier?"

"*Oui.*"

Glancing at Erick, I lift my hands in frustration.

He nods. "Details, CC. Full report."

As CC takes his duties more seriously, his heavy French accent nearly evaporates. "Marcus

Frazier disappeared from our records entirely approximately five years ago. After communicating with various regional outposts, I discovered the reason. He died in a suspicious fire in Québec City."

"Suspicious how?" My wheels are turning.

CC continues. "Initially, the fire was ruled accidental. However, a hotshot new arson investigator reopened several cases when he joined the force in Québec. Reexamining the evidence resulted in a most tantalizing *pomme de terre* discovery."

Scrunching up my face, I stare at Erick in confusion.

He grins. "It's French for potato, Moon. I'd think someone with your proclivities would know the word for potato in every language."

Proclivity and potatoes get me giggling.

CC laughs lightly. "I must hear more of these proclivities, *Mademoiselle* Moon."

"Not likely, CC. Please continue." Despite my bravado, my cheeks flush. Something about a man in uniform. And I've seen this Canadian Mountie in all his red-coated glory.

Erick snaps his fingers in front of my face and shakes his head. My cheeks redden further, but I refuse to out myself.

CC continues. "The fire, along with five others, was set using a lit cigarette and a bag of chips."

Both of my hands land on the dented desk.

"Chips? You mean potato chips, right? Someone started a fire using a bag of potato chips?"

"*Oui*. A diabolical device. The energy contained in the fats, starches, and proteins burns hot and for plenty of time to start trouble. It is truly ingenious—in a terrible way."

My eyes lock onto Erick's. "You have to get me back into that arena, Sheriff."

CC chuckles softly on his end of the phone. "I must say my goodbyes before I become embroiled in your lover's quarrel. I bid you *adieu, Mademoiselle* Moon."

"Yeah, catch you later, CC."

He laughs as the call ends, and Erick taps a pencil violently against his desk. "I need to call the fire chief this time. Poking around to see if the trophy was missing was one thing. But we'll be walking in there hoping to uncover the flash point and the mechanism of this arson-caused fire. It has to be official, Moon."

"Fine by me. The more, the merrier." Leaning back against the seat, I cross my arms and shake my head. "I can't believe I missed it. Pyewacket has dragged the bag of potato chips out of the cupboard in the back room three times in the last two days. I'm not one to complain about potato chips, so I eat a few handfuls and put the bag away every time. I almost don't need to visit the scene, but I'd like to confirm this hunch with my own senses."

Erick checks the phone to make sure the call has been disconnected, leans forward, and grins. "You mean your extra senses?"

"Can confirm."

CHAPTER 17

TURNS OUT, a sudden fire in the dead of winter hadn't been sitting well with the fire chief. When Erick requests permission to revisit the scene with his honorary deputy—I'm sure we all remember that debacle—we're granted instant approval.

As we exit the vehicle and approach the rubble, it's clear to even a barely local like myself that a brutal winter storm is brewing. The temperature has plummeted well below zero, and the Arctic wind knifing across the great lake means business.

I tug a hat from the pocket of my coat and pull it down over my ears. Erick takes my mittened hand, flicks on a powerful flashlight, and leads the way to the area that once served as the first-floor lounge.

My only previous experience visiting a burned-out building was unescorted, and that ended about as badly as you might imagine, but that's another story. Time to focus up. Erick is giving me the lay of the land.

"So, there would've been a bank of windows here, looking out on the sheets. You can see the husks of the vending machines there."

I glance around the room and beg my moody mood ring for a sliver of assistance. "And where would the side table and the ashtray have been?"

He circles a blackened shape on the ground, orients himself, and points with the flashlight. "There. You can roughly see the outline of what would've been the end table. They took the ashtray and samples from the surrounding area into the—"

"Look!"

Erick shifts the flashlight to my face, and I'm instantly blinded. "Hey! Stop. Stop."

He flicks the beam to the floor. "Sorry. I thought you were in trouble. What are you looking at?"

Inching forward, I crouch near the blackened shapes on the floor. Slipping off my mitten, I point in silence.

Erick moves in and trains the light to the area I'm indicating. "Looks like all the rest of the ashes to me, Moon. Are you getting some kind of message?"

I wasn't, but as soon as he says the word, the ring on my left hand turns to a circle of ice inside my glove. I slide my hand out and search the smoky cabochon.

An image of Ridgely's Barbecue Potato Chips wavers in the mist. "I am now. That's not just any ash, Erick. It's melted plastic—or whatever they make potato chip bags from. We need to get a sample of that and compare it to a bag of Ridgely's Barbecue Potato Chips."

Erick makes a low groaning sound.

I look up and shrug. "What? Is there something bad about Ridgely's? Is that not a real brand?"

"It's a Canadian brand. The only reason they're able to get it here is because we're so close to the border. A lot of folks in town prefer it."

Slowly getting to my feet, a claircognizant knowing consumes me for several moments.

"Mitzy?" Erick snaps his fingers in front of my face. "Mitzy, what is it?"

"If you check with CC, I guarantee you the arsonist used Ridgely's in every one of those six fires in Canada, including the one that killed Marc Frazier."

Erick rubs my shoulder and nods. "I'll call him tomorrow. But as far as I'm concerned, it's fact. You've never let me down before, Moon."

A chill runs down my spine, and I shake involuntarily. "I think I know why Kurt is so terrified."

My protective boyfriend scoops an arm around

my shoulders. "Let's hop back in the cruiser and turn the heater on. I need to call the fire chief and get someone out here to collect the samples. You can tell me what you think is scaring Kurt once I get you out of the elements."

On the radio with the fire station, Sheriff Harper promises to hold the scene until the fire investigator shows up. The chief is pleased that there might be a break in the arson case. So pleased, in fact, he promises Erick a pint at Final Destination. The sheriff politely accepts the invitation, but I doubt very seriously he'll make good on it.

Once he signs off, I say as much. "Are you actually going to go to that bar and have a drink with the fire chief?"

"Sure. Why wouldn't I?"

Turning in the seat, I stare in momentary shock. "I don't know. I thought you always went straight home to check on your mom after work. Do you go out drinking without me? Often?"

He leans forward and rests his head on the steering wheel as he chuckles softly. "Oh boy. We're not even hitched yet and you're already putting the kibosh on boys' night."

My eyes widen. "It's a regular thing? There's a name for it?"

He turns, and his mischievous blue eyes twinkle. "There's a lot you don't know about me, Moon, but I'm an open book. Ask me anything."

"All right. Is this boys' night actually a thing?"

He sniffs and shrugs. "Technically, yes. In reality, it only works out every few months. It's just a group of deputies, firefighters, paramedics, the chief, and me. With the hours we all keep, the group is generally pretty thin. Although, I enjoy myself when I'm able to make it."

I nod my head slowly. Wow! It's not that I mind he has a boys' night, it's that I mind being reminded of how little I know about this man. "Got it. Boys' night: check. Now, what else do I need to know?"

He smirks, and I pick a phrase out of the air. "Middle name. Good idea. What's your middle name, Harper?"

A self-satisfied grin splits his face in two. "I don't have one. Erick Harper is my full and legal name."

"What? You don't have a middle name? Why?"

"I just don't. My mother gave me a unique first name and of course, her last name, but she didn't feel the need to burden me with any other baggage. So it's Erick Harper. Plain and simple."

The shock and awe steal my voice. How can I be dating a man, dreaming of being engaged to said man, and not know his whole name? I'm the worst! "All right. What about your birthday? Why have you never told me the day of your birth? I'm starting to feel like a terrible girlfriend! I can't believe I never got you a birthday present, Erick 'No Middle Name' Harper. When is your birthday?"

He's gripped by a fit of laughter, and the cloud of his breath hangs in the slowly warming air inside the vehicle. That heater is definitely slacking.

"My birthday is April 1st, Moon."

"Oh, come on! Now you're making things up."

He shakes his head and places a hand over his heart. "I swear on my life. My birthday is on April Fools' Day. The reason I don't talk about it is that look on your face right there. No one ever believes me. I always try to explain myself. In the end, everyone thinks it's a hilarious joke. My mother tried to throw birthday parties for me a few times after I entered elementary school, but no one ever showed up. They figured it must be a big April Fools' joke."

The energy inside the patrol car shifts to sadness. For a moment, I can see the little boy inside the grown man. He's alone at a table filled with decorations, and candles flickering on a cake. Rather than cheers, tears trickle down his cheek as his mother blows out the candles.

I lurch across the vehicle and hug him tightly. "I'm so sorry. I'm going to make sure you have the best birthday party in the world! Every year for as long as I live!"

He rubs his hand on my stocking hat and kisses my forehead. "Any birthday I get to spend with you will be the best birthday I've ever had."

Just when things are about to get ridiculously mushy, headlights swipe across the parking lot as someone turns in.

Erick hops out of the vehicle and waves his arms.

The car drives toward us, stops with the headlights on about twenty yards off, and someone steps out of the vehicle.

As I open my door to share my great findings with the fire investigator, a shot rings out, and Erick falls.

The silhouetted figure thunders across the parking lot, grabs me by the back of the coat, and drags me kicking and screaming toward his vehicle. Within seconds, I'm in the trunk, and we are fishtailing away from the arena.

I didn't see what happened to Erick.

I didn't get to tell him my theory about Kurt's fears.

And I never got a chance to say goodbye.

CHAPTER 18

As the frigid air seeps into the metal trunk, my first instinct is to weep uncontrollably. Not for myself, but for my fallen hero. Is Erick alone—bleeding out in the snow? Maybe the actual fire investigator got there in time, but in time for what?

Fortunately, my unhealthy relationship with danger has taught me survival is based on quick thinking and action, not pity. Time to stuff these emotions way down with the rest.

Reaching into the pocket of my coat, I extract my phone and text Erick. I can't risk a call. My captor might overhear.

No reply.

The torrent of tears threatens to break through.

Next, I text Paulsen. "Erick shot. Arena parking lot. Arsonist in Pin Cherry. I'm in his trunk."

Holding the phone to my chest, I confirm the volume is off and wait. There's a quick vibration, and my eager eyes search the screen for Erick's name.

No joy.

The reply is from Paulsen. It simply states, "10-4."

The man in the driver's seat places a call. His thick cockney accent is unfamiliar, and I wonder if I've tripped and fallen into a *Lock, Stock and Two Smoking Barrels* sequel. My abductor sounds exactly like Jason Statham.

Not knowing where the car is headed or what the outcome of this unfortunate kidnapping will be, I text Silas a brief description of my circumstances and ask him to inform Grams.

I expect no response. He's told me on more than one occasion that he abhors the idea of texting.

It's a testament to his love for me that I actually receive a reply. "You possess the skills to survive. Use everything you have learned. I will assist Erick in finding you."

As I type what little I know of Erick's current situation and the unlikelihood of him finding me, the tears break through my defenses. The cold is seeping into my bones, and my teeth are chattering as I weep. I barely notice the vehicle slide to a halt.

I've totally lost track of time, but fortunately, my mood ring burns an urgent message.

An image of my cell phone.

Right!

This chimney sweep of a captor will certainly search me once he removes me from the trunk. Assuming he's *going to* remove me from the trunk. Either way, leaving my phone on and stashing it somewhere in here is my only chance to help the people looking for me.

Using my phone to illuminate the tight quarters, I lift a corner of the floor panel beneath me and slide my phone into a hidey-hole.

Wrapping my arms around my shuddering torso, I wait for Phase 2 of this dangerous debacle.

Heavy footsteps tromp through the snow outside the car, and I'm reminded of a special I once watched on Foley artists. I still remember how they used packets of dried milk to mimic the sound of a polar bear's feet on the ice pack. The approaching crunch gets louder with each step. The trunk pops open, and strong hands yank me to my feet.

"Don't gimme any trouble, girlie. 'And over your mobile or I'll knock your lights out 'fore you knows what's hit ya."

"I don't have a phone. I left it at home on the charger. Search me if you want." I paint my features into the portrait of innocence.

"We'll see if 'at bit flies." He carelessly pats me down and spits on the dirty snow.

I desperately search the horizon for a landmark. Nada. Bupkus.

Although, with my phone in the trunk of this hooligan's car . . .

He had called someone to report he had "the bird in the boot." So I'm expecting to meet his boss at any moment. I struggle to formulate a plan as he drags me into a warehouse near the edge of the frozen lake and clicks a pair of handcuffs around my wrists.

"No funny business, Dolly."

I refuse to answer and shuffle my feet as slowly as possible.

An industrial metal door creaks open, and he shoves me further into a dank, greasy space lit by two single bulbs dangling overhead from extension cords. Crates, fifty-five-gallon drums, and an enormous shipping container fill the space. My senses detect a presence in the shadows.

"So pleased you chose to drop by, Mizithra."

It can't be. The hairs on the back of my neck stand on end, and my stomach roils with fear. That slimy, arrogant voice can only belong to one person.

"I shall take your silence as recognition. My doctors tell me I was incredibly lucky to regain my memory. Such a long road to recovery."

Any shadow of doubt vanishes. Somehow, Frank Freeman, a.k.a. Rory Bombay, has returned.

"After the severe head injury, which stole my memories, I'm sure you and your precious Sheriff Harper thought you'd seen the last of Rory Bombay."

He blames the severe injury, which hopefully means he has no idea my amateur alchemy skills played a part in his demise. "Wishful thinking, I guess, Frank." In the past, the use of his true name always threw him a little off his game.

His wicked laugh echoes through the warehouse. "I'm so sorry, my dear. Those little tricks will no longer be effective. Through my months and months of recovery, Frank Freeman and I came to an understanding. He is weak, spineless, and has no chance for success. Gaining our freedom and returning to our rightful place could only be handled by Mr. Bombay."

"Likely story." Creep factor: high!

A stony silence hangs in the air. "In the end, Frank took very little convincing. He retreated to his dark corner and relinquished all control to me. I had plenty of time to read, study, and rebuild my stores of knowledge—among other things."

"What is this about, Frank? Why would you burn down a hockey arena? It hardly seems on par with the rare magical items that you generally look to add to your collection."

"Ah, you know me so well, Mizithra. Unfortunately, my brief stay in the sanatorium had a devastating impact on my fortunes—and my collections. Once Frank retreated, and I was able to move forward with rebuilding my empire, I knew I needed capital."

The urge to call him a deviant sociopath, and tackle him—WWE-style—is building.

"Extensive research into local legends and scandals led me to the perfect solution. A solid gold trophy that would serve me well."

"Well, kudos to you. You've got the trophy. See ya." I nod my head dismissively.

Bombay continues without skipping a beat. "I met the brother of this fine man beside you, Mr. Gammon, in the psychiatric rehabilitation facility I was visiting. When I learned their family story and how a solid gold championship trophy had been stolen from their grandfather's team, I tracked down Gammon and made him an offer he couldn't refuse. Isn't that right, old boy?"

"Yeah, I told ya, guv, I'd do anyfink to get 'at trophy. Den't I?" Once again, the thug spits on the ground.

"Indeed, you did. And you've held up your end of the bargain nicely, Gammon. Could you see to the arrangements in Mizithra's sleeping quarters? She and I need a moment alone."

As soon as Gammon heads into the shipping container, I remove the handcuffs from my wrists using the technique Silas taught me. They drop to the floor with a clang, and I place one hand on my hip. "This is not going to end like you plan, Frank."

His throaty chuckle is unsettling. "I have new powers of my own now, Mizithra. I took up jewelry making at the facility. The combination of a chunk of rare meteorite and my addition of certain ancient runes created an astonishingly potent item." A single hand reaches into the light, and his dangerous ring emits a dull reddish glow.

Using another of Silas's teachings, I close my extra senses off and focus on resistance. "I'm no damsel in distress. I should think you would've learned I can take care of myself."

Bombay grumbles under his breath and withdraws the ringed hand. He crosses his arms over his chest, and as he steps into the light, his devious green eyes twinkle. "Point of fact, you've never actually saved yourself, have you? And I should think you've learned that reliance on friends is your greatest weakness. Sheriff Harper will not be coming to your rescue this time, will he, Mizithra?"

At the mention of Erick, my heart shudders. Rory must've given his lackey specific instructions to take out the sheriff. If this truly is to be my last stand, I'm going to make sure Frank Freeman, a.k.a. Rory Bombay, gets exactly what he has coming to him. "So you tricked Kurt into stealing the trophy for you and then you tried to kill him by burning the whole place down. Congratulations on failing. What's your new plan?"

"I hate to inform you, Miss Moon. Kurt was quite successful at stealing the trophy. And I had no intention of killing him in the fire. His forced confession was exactly the thing that pushed you and your misguided Romeo back to the scene of the crime. No new plan needed."

"You knew I would go back?" My spine stiffens, and cold tendrils creep across my back.

He snickers. "You are nothing if not predictable." Rory steps closer and points. "In fact, now that you've successfully removed your handcuffs, I'm certain you imagine overpowering me and escaping."

I'm sure he can't read minds, but that came close. "Hardly. I'm actually pretty curious to see what part you think I'll play in this foolish scheme."

Rory grabs a handful of my hair and pulls me close enough for me to choke on the scent of his pricey cologne. "You have always been the plan. You're my payday and my ticket out of this godforsaken county."

"Payday? I thought you said Kurt got you the trophy." His nearness is making my skin crawl, and I need to get away.

"Ah, yes. Kurt was so successful, in fact, that he stole it twice. The one he brought to me was a cheap imitation. Not worth the cherrywood base it stood on."

So, that was the truth within Kurt's lie. "He really threw the original into the lake?"

At last, Rory shoves me away and paces. "Emotion is such a pitiful crippler. I'm pleased to report I suffer no such deficiency." He turns toward me and sneers. "The Duncan-Moon Foundation will fund my activities for as long as I deign to keep you alive. You are my new trophy, Mizithra Achelois Moon."

This is the part in every *Scooby Doo* episode where Fred or Velma inform the villain they'll never get away with it. Why mess with a classic? "You'll never get away with it, Frank. Deputies are already en route."

Fury bubbles to the surface, and Rory bellows, "Gammon! You didn't take her phone? You bumbling idiot. Search the car at once!"

Gammon slinks out of the shipping container, avoids eye contact, and heads for the door. The now familiar opening creak echoes through the structure and—

"Hands in the air. The Birch County sheriffs

have the place surrounded. Where's Miss Moon?" Deputy Paulsen's emotionless voice booms through a bullhorn.

I open my mouth to scream out a reply, but firm hands restrain me and cover my mouth.

"Looks like I'll be cashing in this ticket sooner than I thought." Rory fishes out his phone and issues a command. "Land the chopper."

"This will never work, Frank. You killed your only chance. Erick would've held his fire to spare me, but Paulsen will take me out as fast as she'll tag you. Big mistake, buddy."

"Lovely fairy story, Mizithra. However, I read all about your gal pal adventures on a canoe trip with Deputy Paulsen. We'll be boarding that chopper in—"

The whir of rotor blades above the warehouse resounds over the docks.

Rory flicks his phone, and his confident voice floods from outdoor speakers.

"Miss Moon and I have a flight to catch. Enjoy your discussions with Mr. Gammon once you have him in custody. If anyone attempts to interfere with our boarding, I will not hesitate to put a bullet in this lovely woman's overactive brain. Understood?"

The silence outside the warehouse is broken only by the whirring helicopter.

Finally, Deputy Paulsen's voice blasts from the

bullhorn. "There's no need to kill the hostage. Tell me your name and what you want in exchange for the hostage."

Yeesh! Didn't she learn that you're supposed to use the hostage's name to humanize the victim?

"I'm hurt you don't recognize me, Deputy. It's your old friend, Rory Bombay."

The helicopter is the only sound.

"My pilot is landing. Please move your perimeter back and do not attempt to interfere." He pushes me forward without waiting for a response.

The lights blind me, and I'm shoved ahead, nothing more than a human shield.

I have no idea if they had time to call in Boomer, the sharpshooter from the Broken Rock sheriff's station, but there's no way I'm getting into that metal bird.

When we reach the halfway point, bathed in the light of the headlights and spots, I quickly hoist both of my feet in the air simultaneously. Without legs to support me, I slip from Rory's grasp and drop to the ground like a sack of cement.

The element of surprise works, and Rory is exposed—for a split second.

A single shot rings out, and Rory Bombay falls backward into the snow.

CHAPTER 19

THE LAST THING I want to do is look at the body sprawled behind me, but I have to get that ring.

Peering through barely open eyelids, I feel for Rory's left hand, yank the ring from his lifeless finger and shove it in my pocket.

The rapid exit of adrenaline from my system hits me in the gut, and I toss my cookies in the snow.

My father beats the paramedics to the scene. Jacob scoops me into his arms and crushes me in a bear hug. "It's over, sweetie. It's really over this time."

I don't remember when I started crying, but sobs wrack my body. I want to tell my father that my whole life is over. That I thought Grams and

Pyewacket were the most important things in my life, but that was before I lost Erick.

My insides feel hollow. An empty shell with an unrelenting heartbeat. A drum being beaten against its will. How can I live without him?

The surrounding scene moves before my eyes in slow motion. Gammon being shoved into the back of a cruiser. Deputies arresting the pilot. Paramedics checking Frank Freeman, calling time of death, and radioing for the medical examiner. The world is still turning, but everything seems one-dimensional. There's nothing special, nothing extra. The fact that I closed off my extrasensory abilities to protect myself from Rory Bombay hardly seems to matter. What good are they now?

The hustle and bustle fade into the background, and the first responders part like the Red Sea as an all-too-familiar shape steps into the light. Haloed by the harsh glow of the headlights, cradling one arm, he walks forward with purpose.

All of my protections evaporate, and the raw, broken bits of my heart swirl together and reform as though the *Planeteers* are creating Captain Planet.

"Erick?"

He attempts to pick up his pace, but winces audibly.

My father loosens his hold and walks me toward the approaching— God, I hope it's not a ghost.

And as though we're simply rehearsing for a wedding, Jacob offers my hand to Erick, and I sob onto the shoulder that's not oozing blood through his shirt. "You're shot. What are you doing walking around? You should be in the hospital!"

He pulls me as close as he can with his good arm and whispers into my neck. "Boomer's on vacation in Alaska. You didn't think I'd let Paulsen run a hostage rescue operation without a sharpshooter, did you?"

My voice catches in my throat, and all I can do is softly cry and watch the dark patch on his other shoulder spread.

"Let's get you home, Moon."

Finally able to accept this new version of reality, I plant my foot in the snow and shake a finger at his stupid, handsome face. "Get yourself in that ambulance right now, Erick 'No Middle Name' Harper. I'm not a damsel in distress. I won't be bossed around by some one-armed bandit."

Laughter grips him, and he presses a hand to his shoulder. "One-armed bandit. Good one, Moon."

Sucking in a deep breath and screwing my courage to the sticking place, I shout to the nearest paramedic. "Get Sheriff Harper to the hospital. This wound is bleeding all over the place."

The medic jogs over and hesitates for a moment. "He said—"

"I don't care what he said. He's shot, and he's going to the hospital. Now get him in an ambulance before I commandeer your vehicle and drive him there myself!"

The nervous man nods and clearly decides I'm the greater threat. He encourages Sheriff Harper to follow him to an ambulance, and I give Erick a helpful push from behind.

As he lies on the gurney, they get him on an IV and take his vitals. I lean over and *whisper-yell* one more time. "Don't you ever scare me like that again, Sheriff Harper. You understand?"

He blinks his dreamy blue eyes and smiles as though he hasn't a care in the world. "Gosh, you're pretty. What's your name, Princess?"

Leaning back, my head snaps to the paramedic. "What did you give him? I thought that was a glucose IV. Is there some type of sedative in there or something for pain?"

The paramedic shakes his head. "Hydration only, ma'am."

The vacant look in Erick's eyes vanishes, and a mischievous sparkle instantly replaces it. "Gotcha, Moon."

"Touché, Harper. Touché." Relief floods through my overwrought system.

We ride in silence to the hospital, and I follow the gurney through the emergency entrance. The nurses transfer Erick to a bed, and they don't protest when I follow the procession through the swinging doors.

"The doctor will be in shortly, Sheriff Harper. There was a stampede at the dairy farm, and we've got multiple casualties."

Erick lifts onto his elbow. "Deaths or injuries?"

My question would've been "cows or people," but I guess that's why Erick is the sheriff.

The nurse places a hand on her chest. "Oh, sorry. Injuries, sir. Two of the hired hands need immediate surgery. But we'll get you up there as soon as possible."

"No rush, miss. I'm stable."

She blushes. "We take care of our heroes, sir."

Now it's my turn. "I'll be sure to alert you if there's any change in his condition."

The petite redhead seems to notice me for the first time. "Oh, right. Sure. Thanks." She backs out and pulls the curtain closed.

"Yeesh! Does everyone in this town fawn over you, Sheriff?" I cross my arms over my chest and pout.

Erick pulls me close with his good arm and whispers, "I prefer a challenge, Moon."

"Happy to be of service." It seems inappropriate to giggle in the emergency room, but this is my life.

A moment of silence hangs between us, and I

know beyond a shadow of a doubt that we're both thinking about the events at the dockside warehouse.

"I'm glad the whole Frank Freeman, a.k.a Rory Bombay business, is over." I draw a shaky breath and exhale loudly.

"I can't believe Freeman escaped that facility without notice. I should've been the first phone call when he turned up missing." Erick scowls.

Now that Erick is a full-fledged member of the inner circle, it's time he learned the truth about Rory Bombay. I lower my voice and move in. "I'm sorry I couldn't tell you this before, but Rory Bombay is about as close to a dark sorcerer as anyone you'll ever meet. He has a collection of powerful ancient magical objects, and he's studied the dark arts more deeply than even Silas, I fear. However, by ignoring the powerful practices of alchemy, not to mention the genuine magic of love freely given, there were some large holes in his training. I'm willing to bet if you call the psychiatric rehabilitation facility, they will report that Frank Freeman is safe in his room. Whether Rory glamoured someone to look like him or simply planted a false memory in the minds of the staff, I can't be sure, but I know he duped them. That's how he always operates. Seduction, lies, duplicitousness, and, ultimately—revenge. I'm glad he'll never bother us again."

Erick looks away and sniffs sharply.

"What is it? What's wrong?"

"I shouldn't have killed him. I didn't have to kill him."

"What are you saying? You had seconds to take that shot. What if he'd been wearing Kevlar? What if you tried to spare his life by shooting him in the leg? You know him! He'd have grabbed me, dragged me to the helicopter, and—"

Erick reaches up with his uninjured arm, and his thumb gently strokes my cheek. "I'm not a murderer."

I grab his hand and get to my feet so quickly that the stupid chair tips over and clatters to the floor. "Murderer? Never! You saved my life. And who knows how many others? You know how his schemes always get out of control. He manipulates innocent people into doing terrible things. The world is a better place without him. I'm sorry you had to pull that trigger, Erick. But, honestly, that's really the point, isn't it? You *had* to pull the trigger."

He turns his head and gazes at the steady drip of the IV.

A nurse enters, glances at the overturned chair, and frowns. "I'll be taking you to surgery now, Mr. Harper."

My world shrinks, and I feel as though I'm fading away as she wheels him from the room.

His arm extending toward the ceiling and offering me a thumbs up as they turn into the hallway is the last thing I see.

I should run into the hall and proclaim my love as they roll him toward the elevators, but my feet are locked in place.

Frozen in fear. Unable to access my gifts.

CHAPTER 20

Cut to—

Welcome to this installment of *I Love Lucy*. Where I'm pacing in the waiting room at the Birch County Regional Medical Facility like a 1950s dad eager for news on the birth of his child.

Erick is in surgery, and I'm losing it. "I swear, it's been days, Silas."

"I can assure you, Mizithra, it has been one and a quarter hours."

"It's been over an hour? Do you think something went wrong? I should go in there! Wait, maybe *you* should go in there!" I nod insinuatingly.

Silas gets to his feet with all the grace and wisdom his age provides. He shuffles toward me and adjusts the pocket square in his fusty tweed coat. Placing a hand on each of my shoulders, he looks deeply into my worried grey eyes. "Sheriff Harper is fine. The mere fact that he was able to attend your rescue and take the shot that assured your safety is a clear indication that the wound is not mortal. For all you know, it was a through-and-through. The surgeon is carefully repairing any damaged blood vessels and ensuring the sheriff heals quickly. Your pacing serves no purpose. Sit with me, and we shall discuss the ring."

At the mention of the powerful magical item in my pocket, my eyes fly open wider than a Betsy Wetsy doll suddenly placed on her feet. "How did you know?"

"An item of that magnitude does not escape my detection."

Silas reaches into a hidden pocket within his coat and extracts a glass container that seems to sparkle strangely in the light.

"What's that made out of?"

He grins proudly. "Your skills are progressing nicely. Most would not notice the subtleties of this vessel. I created a special recipe for blowing my own glass. There are unique minerals contained in the formula that interfere with the energy of magical items. It is not a permanent solution, but it will shield us while we study this item."

As I retrieve the ring from my left pocket, a nasty oozing sensation tickles my fingertips, and I swear it's emitting dangerous whispers.

Silas scoops the glass container under my fingers and taps my hand to release the item. He frowns and shakes his head. "I pray those precious moments in your pocket will have no ill effect in the future."

"What? I didn't feel anything until I pulled it out. I swear!"

He harrumphs and smooths his bushy grey mustache. I lean closer, and we hunch over the item as he turns it within its glass prison. "The item itself is quite ancient. I must compare the markings to those in one of my texts when I return to my home, but I believe it may be Phoenician—or perhaps a surviving artifact from the Library of Alexandria. Priceless. A true treasure."

Tilting my head, I search for the right words. "Are you— Is it something— Would you be giving this to a museum? It's gotta be dangerous. Rory said he 'added' something to it."

"Ah, if I am able to erase the wicked stain from its noble core, then that is exactly what I shall do. If, however, Mr. Bombay's working is too severely intertwined with the object, I shall protect and preserve the artifact in my vault."

There's no safer place on earth. I've seen and felt the power of the alchemical protections surrounding it. "It's quite an interesting piece. I hope you can clear it—or whatever you call it."

"Indeed." He places the shimmering vial in my hand and continues, "Your powers will be severely limited by the ingredients in the glass itself. However, use what you have at your disposal and tell me what impressions you receive from the item. It will aid me greatly if I have a better understanding of the magics that have been applied."

Taking a deep breath to still my stuttering heart and fried nerves, I open up my extrasensory perceptions and hope to receive a message from one of them.

Almost immediately, a small phrase floats through the air. "I hear the phrase 'power over.'"

Silas nods sadly. "That should not surprise us. Mr. Bombay made a lifelong study of manipulating the free will of others. Continue."

Replaying the small memory clip of the tingles in my fingers as I removed the item from my pocket, I pull additional information. An icy chill stabs between my shoulder blades and I shake violently. "Oh, Silas. It's so much worse than we imagined."

He removes the jar from my hand and slips it inside his coat. "Tell me."

"It's like he took all the enchantments he's tried

separately and blended them into one hideous master spell. The ring gives him the power to convince anyone he talks to of anything he says. And it somehow simultaneously makes the listener feel indebted or— It creates a sycophant. Does that make sense?"

My mentor nods and exhales with effort. "Anything else?"

"Actually, yeah. There seems to be a component that is in a constant state of premonition. No, that's not right. It's like it gives him the ability to see into the future—not super far—but a few minutes at a time."

Silas nods and strokes his mustache. "Interesting. Focus on that component and see if you can draw any additional details."

"You got it."

Sinking into the chair, I take another deep breath, but what I see is cloudy. "I can't get it— Hold on! I figured it out!" Turning toward Silas, I feel relief for the first time since that initial gunshot outside the burned-out hockey arena. "He was trying to create clairvoyance from magic and manipulation. But he couldn't get it quite right, and the information he saw was clouded. So, he had some knowledge of what would happen a few minutes in the future, but he couldn't always get the right info. Kind of like when my mood ring shows me something, but it doesn't make sense right away. You know what I mean?"

He nods. "I know exactly what you mean, Mizithra. Thank you. This information will assist me greatly in undoing what has been done."

"Do you think he knew that he was going to be shot?"

"I do not. As you have experienced, when emotions run high, it is difficult to receive information. I believe if Mr. Bombay had known the outcome of forcing you toward the helicopter, he would've chosen a different exit. Would you not agree?"

Oh brother. Yes, I would not agree? No, I would not agree? You'd think after all of this time with Silas as my mentor, I'd have gotten over my disdain for that phrasing. "I'm sure you're right."

A concerned doctor walks toward us, and my heart feels like a lead balloon in my chest.

I can't breathe, and I'm struggling to read the expression on the surgeon's face. Of course, the panic interferes with my abilities.

"Is he all right? Can I see him?"

The stoic doctor offers a perfunctory smile. "He's in recovery. The surgery went well. We recovered the bullet and repaired the damage. He should be ready to see you in about half an hour."

Silas places a hand on the doctor's arm, and the

intimate gesture seems unusually familiar for my stalwart alchemist.

"Thank you, doctor. I'm certain it would bring great comfort to Mr. Harper if Miss Moon were there when he opens his eyes. I'm sure you understand."

A strange energy hums in the air, and I smile despite the situation. What of your precious ethics, Mr. Willoughby? I'd never say it out loud! But I can entertain a brief, silent moment of moral superiority.

The expression on the surgeon's face shifts, and he glances toward me. "If you'll follow me, Miss Moon. I'll take you back to the recovery area."

Silas slips a book from his coat and presses it into my hand.

As I walk toward the swinging doors, a step behind the doctor, I glance over my shoulder and offer a confused grin to Silas.

A broad smile pushes up the corners of his bushy mustache.

However, the grin quickly fades from my face when the doctor slides the curtain back and gestures toward a stiff plastic chair beside Erick's bed.

Nothing could have prepared me for this tableau.

My strong, independent boyfriend lies limp in the hospital bed. An IV stand beside the head of the bed holds two bags feeding into a single tube heading toward a patch of tape on his forearm. His skin is pale, and a cannula feeds oxygen through his nostrils.

The doctor exits and pulls the curtain closed behind him.

I collapse into the chair beside Erick's bed and blink rapidly to hold back the torrent of tears building behind my eyelids.

Reaching for his hand, I cradle it gently in mine. I've never seen him look so weak and helpless. There's no sign of the man who stood up after being shot in the shoulder, climbed to the roof of a warehouse adjacent to where I was being held captive, and fired a sniper rifle with deadly accuracy.

The silence, broken only by the beeping of the machines, is unbearable. I glance at the book in my hand. *Great Expectations*. Clearly, Silas meant for me to read to Erick.

The minutes tick away with the lazy attitude of a coed on spring break. My mouth is speaking the words on the page, but my mind drifts off to create a variety of scenarios where Erick is spared the bullet that put him in this hospital bed.

Charles Dickens continues, "In a word, I was too cowardly to do what I knew to be right . . ."

As I create alternate script number four, a weak

flicker pulses through the fingers in his hand, and I turn toward him eagerly.

His expression is soft and dreamy. Erick seems trapped between the world of anesthesia and the world I occupy.

"Hey, Moon."

The sound of his voice breaks the waterworks loose. Tears sluice down my cheeks, and I squeeze his hand relentlessly. "Don't you ever scare me like that again, Erick Harper."

The crispness returns to his gaze, and he squeezes my hand a little harder. "Looks like the shoe's on the other foot this time, eh?"

I lurch forward, the book falls to the floor, and I hug him.

He winces in pain. "Easy on the shoulder, Moon."

"Sorry. Sorry. I'm so happy that you're awake, I forgot."

He chuckles and groans simultaneously. "You forgot that the reason I'm in this hospital bed is that I took a bullet in the shoulder? What did you think I was doing here?"

"Touché." Our laughter lightens the mood, and I squeeze his hand in both of mine.

"How did you know that was my favorite book?"

Apparently, *Great Expectations* is his favorite

book. Yet another thing I didn't know about him. "Never mind that. Are you even going to feel up to attending the Yuletide Extravaganza thingy tomorrow night?"

At the mention of the extravaganza, his whole body stiffens. Instantly, there's an image of the snow princess in my brain.

"What happened? Do you not want to go? I mean, we can totally skip it."

He attempts to cover his discomfort with a cough. "I'll be fine. It's fine. They'll release me in the morning, and we'll hit the mulled cider booth tomorrow night. Deal?"

Scrunching up my face, I size up the sheriff. "You're up to something. I don't like it when you're being sneaky."

"Really? So you're the only one allowed to get into trouble or plan to get into trouble?"

Whatever he's hiding from me, he's doing an excellent job. Once again, I suspect he's received tutelage from Silas. "Because you're injured, I'm not going to fight you. Although, let the record show, I'm suspicious."

He grins proudly. "You wouldn't be Mitzy Moon if you weren't. Now go home and get some sleep. I'm not the only one who's been through an ordeal."

"You're not wrong." I exhale and let my shoulders relax. "I'm going to stay here until they kick me out. And then I'm going to bring you breakfast in the morning. Blueberry pancakes from the diner. You're not gonna eat any crappy hospital food on my watch."

Erick squeezes my hand and brings my fingers to his lips. "Tell you what. You stay until they kick you out, and then I'll meet you at the diner for breakfast. How's that sound?"

"Sounds amazing. Are you sure you'll be up to it?"

"Absolutely. I've got a lot motivating me." He looks directly into my eyes and squeezes my hand.

Uh oh! These aren't the right kind of tingles for a hospital room. Maybe I should head out sooner rather than later. Quick, I need a distraction. Retrieving the book from the floor, I place it on the side table.

"I'm more exhausted than I thought. I burned through a lot of adrenaline pacing out there in the waiting room."

He laughs and grimaces. "No jokes, Moon. I'm supposed to be resting. Remember?"

"Copy that. See you at Myrtle's in the morning, all right?"

He squints his eyes and appears confused. "Come a little closer. I don't think I heard you clearly."

"Oh, sure." As I innocently lean in, Erick quickly plants a kiss on my surprised mouth.

"I love you, Mitzy Moon."

Blinking back another wave of tears, I kiss his pale, pouty mouth. "And I love you."

CHAPTER 21

Wandering from the recovery area, a sense of peace washes over me. A huge threat to my safety has been removed, and Erick is going to be all right. At least physically. I'm sure we'll have a few more discussions about the psychological impact of what happened tonight, but I stand by my reasoning. There was no option. I'm grateful to be alive, and the first person I need to share that gratitude with is Grams. She's going to be furious with me for almost getting killed.

Pushing the doors to the waiting room open, it dawns on me that I rode here in the ambulance. It's probably only a mile or two walk back to my book-shop, but at this time of year, in the dead of night, I'm likely to turn into a human ice statue before I make it three blocks.

I pull out my phone and glance at the time. Shoot! It's after midnight. I could call my dad, but—

"Perhaps I could offer you transport to your bookshop, Mizithra."

"Silas? Have you been waiting this whole time?"

"Indeed. You had no transport of your own, and regardless of your powers of persuasion, I felt certain the night nurse would force you to leave at some point. I had no previous commitments, so I chose to delay my departure."

Leave it to Silas to make hanging around waiting to give me a ride sound like *The Da Vinci Code*. "Thank you. I was already twisting my brain into knots, trying to figure out who to call."

His cheeks redden. "I believe it is appropriate for one to call the Ghostbusters." He's barely able to complete his retort before guffaws grip him.

"Oh boy! If you're pulling out pop culture references, it's way past your bedtime, Silas. You're as punchy as a preteen at a sleepover. Let's hit the road."

As we traverse the frozen tundra that is the parking lot, my eyes fall on my mentor's Model T. Whoops! For a hot minute, I'd forgotten what he drives.

Sensing my unease, Silas reassures me. "Never

fear. I have sufficient woolen blankets to keep you warm on the drive."

I offer a silent "Yippee" and climb into the passenger seat. He turns the crank as necessary and joins me inside the frosty Ford.

"I am certain your grandmother will be most interested in hearing the details of tonight's near catastrophe."

"You betcha."

Again Silas chuckles. "You are becoming more and more the local with each passing day, Mizithra. Will I be seeing you tomorrow night at the extravaganza?"

"Yeah, Erick said he'll be up to it. Which reminds me, have you been secretly tutoring him?"

A smug look grips his wizened features.

And an image of a snow princess dances in my head. "No need to answer, Silas. Whatever you two are planning, I'm not pleased."

He chuckles under his breath. "Then I shall see you tomorrow evening."

The alchemist stops at the end of the alley, and I impulsively lean across and kiss his jowly cheek. "Thank you for always being there for me, Silas. And especially, thanks for getting me in that room to see Erick as soon as possible. You really are the best lawyer I've ever had."

He pats my knee firmly. "I believe it is fair to say I am the only lawyer you've ever had."

"Doesn't mean it's not true." Popping out of the vehicle, I cautiously jog toward the side entrance and grin as his jalopy sputters into the night.

If you were expecting a half-ghost, half-feline welcoming committee, you're correct. The second I open the door, Grams lights into me as Pyewacket vocalizes his concern in the background.

"Easy! Easy. I'm fine. Erick's fine. Let me get into my pajamas, and I promise to tell you everything."

"And you nearly scared me to death, young lady."

Holding up a finger, I grin. "Technically—"

"Oh, don't you get smart with me. You know exactly what I mean. Hustle upstairs and spill!"

I manage to take a full stride before Pyewacket blocks my path and drops a bag of potato chips at my feet.

Crouching, I stroke his proud head. "Yes. As usual, you are the true super sleuth. The fire was one hundred percent arson, and it was absolutely started with a bag of potato chips. I have additional details on that as well."

"Reeeee-ow." A warning.

"Give me a second to get changed, son."

"RE-OW!" Game on! Pye bolts up the staircase

with speed and grace. I follow at a slow, measured pace designed to preserve my life.

It only takes a moment for me to slip into my reindeer onesie pajamas and collapse onto a comfortable mound of pillows atop my blessed bed.

Pyewacket leaps directly onto my chest, and Grams hovers above me like a ghost possessed.

"Don't you dare fall asleep! You promised to spill the beans. Now spill!"

With difficulty, I push myself to a low-angle sitting position without disturbing his royal furriness. "All right. First off, Kurt Frazier is completely innocent of the arson. However, he did steal the trophy."

Grams rockets toward the ceiling. "I knew it. Like father, like son."

"Not exactly. Kurt didn't steal the trophy recently. He stole it over a decade ago and tossed it through a fishing hole in the ice. Gone forever. He replaced it with a remarkable copy, and no one noticed any change. It's not like people are testing the trophies on the daily."

Grams zooms back down and hovers at eye level. "Who on earth would throw away a solid gold trophy?"

I shrug. "Apparently, he'd had it up to his eyeballs with his dad's hijinks. He'd taken a lot of bullying for the questionable incident surrounding the 1975 curling championship and had blindly defended his dad for way too long. He placed all the blame on the trophy, and I guess he thought getting rid of it would solve his problems."

"Are you saying he thought the trophy itself was cursed?"

"Not sure. I think it was more like the impulsive actions of an angry son."

"Well, then it must've been Marc Frazier himself making a second attempt. But why would he leave his own son to die in a fire?"

"Wrong again, Ghost-lock Holmes."

"Mitzy, you're a riot."

"Unfortunately, Marc Frazier fell victim to a serial arsonist about five years ago."

Grams clutches her pearls. "Oh, my."

"Any guess what this arsonist's signature might be?"

Ghost-ma throws her ethereal limbs in the air and shakes her head. "I have no idea, dear. Don't keep me in suspense."

Pyewacket gazes up at me knowingly and seems to wink.

"Correct, Robin Pyewacket Goodfellow. I see your powers of deduction survived your reincarnation."

"Reow." Can confirm.

"Mr. Gammon sets all of his fires using a bag of Ridgely's Barbecue Potato Chips."

Grams reaches a glowing limb toward her spoiled feline and runs her fingers along his back. He rumbles with happiness, and I continue. "Erick got a bunch of info from his Canadian Mountie buddy. Sounds like this Gammon character set about six fires in Canada. Bad news is, Rory Bombay—"

Grams screeches like a harpy. "Don't say that name in my presence."

"Um, I hate to be the one to tell you, but Frank Freeman escaped from the psychiatric facility. Memories intact."

"Nooooo!" Ghost-ma is so panicked she nearly fades from existence.

"Calm down, Isadora. He met Gammon's brother in the facility and learned all about the fires, the mechanism, and I'm pretty sure Marc Frazier's untimely death. And, as only Rory Bombay can do, he manipulated innocent, and guilty, people into doing his bidding. We have to confirm with Kurt, but Rory claims he made Kurt steal the trophy. Not knowing it was a fake, of course. Then, to tie up loose ends, also as usual, he had Gammon knock out Kurt and set the arena on fire."

Grams is shaking her head in horror. "Oh, that poor Kurt. I'm so glad you and Amaryllis arrived in time. What about Gammon? How did Rory plan to tighten up that loose end?"

Gulp. This is the part of the story I was dreading.

"Young lady, what on earth happened to you?"

As quickly as possible, I tell her my terrible tale. The gunshot, the trunk of the car, the face-to-face with Rory, the revealing of the ring, Gammon used as the sacrificial lamb, and the unbelievable rescue.

You're correct in assuming she interrupts me multiple times, but I felt it would be simplest for all of us to "cut to" the enormous lecture I'm receiving now.

"What on earth were you thinking, Mizithra Achelois Moon? That handsome Erick almost died for you."

"I'm sorry. I know how upset you get when handsome people are injured or, worse yet, killed."

"I'm ignoring your sass. That man is an angel come to earth."

"He is. You're right. He's gonna be fine. No complications. Recovering nicely. And he's still planning on taking me to the extravaganza to-morrow night."

At the mention of the extravaganza, Pyewack-et's black-tufted ears twitch, and Grams falls un-usually silent.

"I knew it! He's up to something, and every-one's in on it. This is the worst!"

Rather than continuing to lecture me, Grams

casually floats into the closet. "You really should focus on your outfit for tomorrow night, dear. You'll be outside for several hours, and you've got to look your best. After all, it is a celebration."

Her tone is so detached it only serves to increase my suspicion. Joining her in the closet, I open my mouth to turn the tables and lecture her. However, something catches my eye.

"What's that pale blue froufrou coat doing in here? That was not in here the last time I came in the closet."

Ghost-ma takes a page from my playbook and attempts innocence. "I'm not sure I know what you mean, sweetie. Everything looks the same to me."

"Myrtle Isadora Johnson Linder Duncan Willamet Rogers, do not make me use my psychic replay to prove that the fake fur coat wasn't here."

She lifts her shimmering fingers in the air and grins. "Fine. Spoil the surprise. Pyewacket and I successfully online shopped. It's meant to be a Christmas present. Don't you just love it?"

Gazing at the giant fluffy coat, I doubt I will even like it. "Thanks, I think."

"Don't judge a book by its cover. Try it on. It's like being hugged by a cloud."

Removing the protective covering, I slide the coat from its padded satin hanger and slip into it.

"Oh, wow! You weren't kidding. This is glorious! I might sleep in it."

Grams rushes toward me in a panic and manages to blast straight through me. Once she reorganizes her discombobulated self, she wags a finger at me. "You wouldn't dare! That coat cost more than my first wedding ring!"

Turning left and right, I gaze at myself in the full-length mirror. My snow-white hair is set off beautifully by the pale blue fur. It even makes my grey eyes shimmer with a hint of blue. "It's not surprising that the coat cost more than your old ring. You could buy diamond rings for a song back in the day."

Her energy ripples oddly, and she immediately changes the subject.

Super *sus*.

"Fabulous. We have your outerwear down. Now, I would suggest white silk-lined ski pants and those white faux fur mukluks. That will be a perfect complement to your gorgeous hair."

"Ski pants? Won't they make the junk in my trunk look even junkier than it already does?"

"Nonsense, they're snug and slimming. You'll look a dream."

She finishes assembling the outfit, complete with white suede mittens over a silk inner lining and rabbit fur earmuffs to match the mukluks.

"All right. That's enough playing dress up for today, Grams. I have to get some sleep and meet Erick at the diner in the morning. Then we'll have to talk to Kurt, interview Gammon, and I'm sure he'll have a mountain of paperwork to get through for the shooting incident."

"Shooting! Why would he have to report his own shooting? Wouldn't the deputy that took him to the hospital write that up?"

Oops. "I kinda skipped the end of my story."

Grams hovers next to Pyewacket, and they shoot dual, disdainful gazes in my direction.

"All right. All right. I was working on finding a way out of the warehouse. I got out of the handcuffs and everything. Then Deputy Paulsen arrived with the cavalry and Rory panicked. He used me as a bargaining chip as he escaped to the helicopter."

I dash into the bathroom and splash water on my face to drown out Ghost-ma's screeching admonitions.

"Sorry, I missed that, Grams. Anyway, I used some of my self-defense training and gave the sniper an opening." My stomach still swirls with discomfort at the memory of the gunshot . . . the sound of Rory's body hitting the snow behind me replays on a sickening loop.

Grams floats toward me, and the energy of her

hand brushes against my cheek. "What aren't you telling me, sweetie?"

"Erick was the sniper."

"The man who'd been shot in the shoulder still came to your rescue? Heaven help me. If I was still alive, I think I'd leave everything in my will to him."

"Grams! Rude!"

She throws her semi-corporeal arms around me and talks through her tears. "I'm only kidding, dear. I just love that man so much."

"Me too. Meeeee too."

CHAPTER 22

THE LAND OF DREAMS holds no peace for me. Sinister figures scurry through the corners of my nightmares, and more than one funeral scene plays out in horrifying detail. By 4:00 a.m. I'm no longer able to pretend that sleep is in the cards.

Grabbing a thick robe and my fuzzy dragon-claw slippers, I tiptoe out to the bookshop. And, for some reason, *Great Expectations* calls to me. I dig through the classics section and snuggle into a cozy reading nook in the children's literature area under the mezzanine.

Earlier at the hospital, I was completely distracted. It feels as though I'm reading the book for the first time. I'm transported to a world where tables can turn in a moment, and the deeper I delve, the more real the scenes become. As the sun gently peeks through the 6 x 6 slumped glass windows at the front of the bookshop, I close my book and breathe deeply.

Life is meant to be lived. Risks are meant to be taken. I feel that in every part of my heart. Sure, I have no interest in running my life that close to the razor's edge on a daily basis, but I'm proud of what Erick and I did.

I'm sorry for the loss of life—legitimately. Regardless of my personal opinions about Rory Bombay, I'm not out to support vigilante justice. Erick was acting in the line of duty, and he did what was necessary to protect innocent civilian life. My opinion on that will not waver.

Time to get myself upstairs, luxuriate in my wonderful steam shower, and pick out the appropriate T-shirt for this morning's breakfast rendezvous.

Grams is waiting for me in the closet when I arrive. "Oh, there you are. I saw you reading earlier, and I didn't want to disturb. Were you having trouble sleeping, sweetie?"

A huge yawn delays my response. "Definitely. A lot of unpleasantness went down, not the least of which was seeing Rory Bombay face-to-face again. Do you think Silas will be able to remove the curse from that ring? It's quite a gorgeous piece, and it definitely belongs in a museum."

"Don't you worry, dear. You and I both know that if there's anyone on this big blue planet who has a prayer of making things right, it's our beloved Silas Willoughby." She takes a lap around the closet, running her ethereal fingers through the fabrics. "Now, which gorgeous little number are you wearing to breakfast?"

Turning from the drawer I've been digging through, I wave the T-shirt in her direction.

She stares, confounded, and then bursts out laughing. "Oh, my stars! That one seems to have been custom-made!"

I tilt the T-shirt toward Pyewacket, who spills lazily across the padded mahogany bench in the center of the closet. He gazes up with one eye.

The phrase at the top of the shirt: "I had my patience tested," sits above an image of an extremely annoyed cat. Beneath that frustrated feline follows the phrase: "I'm negative."

Pyewacket blinks once, twitches his tufted ears, and places his powerful jaw on top of his left paw.

"Maybe he doesn't get the joke, Grams."

"Oh, I doubt that, sweetie. I happen to think he sees no reason to state the obvious. You have no patience. We're all quite aware."

Chuckling as I get changed, I have to agree. "Well, patience or not, I'm living my best life in Pin Cherry Harbor. I wouldn't change a thing."

Grams floats behind me as I move into the bathroom to splash cold water on my face and run a comb through my hair.

She hovers in the doorway and grins. "Not one thing? You wouldn't change one little thing? Interesting."

The hairs on the back of my neck stand on end. Again, I feel a conspiracy swirling through the town. Shades of *Something Wicked This Way Comes*, but less malevolent.

PING.

"It's Erick. He's already there! I can't believe I was incapable of getting to the diner ahead of my wounded boyfriend. Yeesh! Gotta go!"

Grabbing my coat and hat from the back of the settee, I hustle down the stairs and out the front door—because I brought my special key this time. Not a fan of jogging, but I can't keep Sheriff Too-Hot-To-Handle waiting at Myrtle's Diner.

As I burst through the door stomping the snow off my feet, Odell offers me the standard spatula salute and nods toward the corner booth.

Erick raises his right hand and starts the process of getting to his feet. I rush forward. "No. No. Sit down. I'm not a Victorian Duchess. You don't have to stand when I walk in, in a T-shirt and jeans."

He chuckles and eases back onto the red vinyl bench seat. I pop off my coat, hang it on the hook at the end of the booth, and shove the hat into the sleeve.

Erick takes one look at me and laughs so hard it obviously hurts. "Come on, Moon. You couldn't have worn a plain white T-shirt? You know I'm supposed to be taking it easy."

Sliding onto the bench seat opposite him, I shake my head. "Oh, so you find something amusing about my T-shirt?"

He grins and makes a yummy growling sound. "I find everything about you fascinating. T-shirts and otherwise."

Head-to-toe tingles, and I haven't even had a cup of coffee.

The world's best waitress, Tally, bobs to the table and slides two steaming mugs of black gold between us. "How you doing there, Sheriff?"

"I should be good as new by the end of the week. Thanks for asking, Tally."

"Word is you took out that good-for-nothing kidnapper with one shot. You did the right thing, Sheriff."

She scurries off to attend to other customers, and I see that faraway look slip into Erick's gaze.

Walking my fingers across the table, I turn up my palm and wait for him to slip his hand into mine. When he does, I squeeze it and smile. "She's right. And I think you'll find the entire town is behind you. People around here know that you're lev-elheaded and fair. No one is ever going to misinterpret the events of last night. You saved my life. Plain and simple."

Erick's gaze returns from that distant place where I can never follow, and he nods slowly. His voice is barely a whisper. "You mean the world to me, you know that, right? And I would do anything to protect you. But it's important for me to say that I would've taken that shot, no matter who Rory was holding hostage."

For a split second I feel jealous, and then a calm acceptance washes over me. "Of course. You were doing your job. You have to protect *all* the citizens of Birch County. Not just me."

Odell approaches the table near the end of that sentence, and once he slides the plates in front of each of us, he places a firm hand on Erick's unin-jured shoulder. "Sheriff Harper, thank you for taking care of this community, and a special thanks for trying to keep this one alive." He jerks a thumb in my direction and grins.

"Look, Gramps, there was a break in the case, and we had to follow up on it. Good news, though, they totally cleared Kurt of the arson."

Odell inhales sharply, raps his knuckles twice on the silver-flecked white Formica, and returns to the kitchen.

As I shake the Tabasco over my breakfast, I ply the sheriff for deets. "Speaking of Kurt, are you bringing him back in for questioning?"

"Won't have to. He's still in a holding cell. He signed that false confession in a heartbeat and hunkered down without complaint. The way I see it, that only further supports your theory that Rory Bombay was threatening him somehow. Regardless, we'll get the full story today. Plus, I'll find out if the curling club wants to press charges for the original theft, and then there'll be a whole international incident to decide who's officially declared the 1975 champs."

My mouth is currently full of perfectly golden home fries, so my ability to make a snarky response is somewhat limited.

Erick shoves a forkful of blueberry pancakes into his mouth and waits for my reply.

A swallow of go-go juice clears the runway. "I'll talk things over with my dad. I don't think we're going to plan on any kind of solid gold trophy, but we can certainly get an appropriate replacement made. Maybe we can mention that when we announce rebuilding the arena."

"Yeah, when's that happening?"

"Shoot! I was gonna text Quince before I got kidnapped. Do you mind if I take care of it right now?"

He lifts a huge bite of pancakes dripping with delicious pure Canadian maple syrup and nods toward my phone.

I fire off a text to Quince and explain the plans to rebuild the arena, replace the trophy, and the need for a fabulous photo op.

A second later, his response comes through, "K."

A fit of giggles grips me. "This kid is never one to waste words." I reply with additional details regarding times, and his simple reply is "2:30."

"Looks like we're on for the photo shoot. I'll get in touch with my dad to make sure he can be there, too."

Erick drains the last of his coffee and smiles. "I'm sure Quince will do a bang-up job. He's about as talented as they come. I have to get into the station and try to make a dent in the paperwork. You want to head over in about fifteen minutes and sit in on the interview with Kurt?"

"Like sit in, sit in? In the interrogation room?"

"Sure. Kurt's comfortable with you, and I think it will make him feel some relief when you tell him what you and your father have planned. I'll get in touch with the curling club and see what their position is before we start the interview. See you in fifteen?"

"Yup."

He slides out of the booth, and the only indication of the immense pain he's feeling is a nearly inaudible wince as he stands.

I want to jump up and pet him like an injured kitten and tell him to go home and get in bed and let me make him some soup. However, Erick Harper is not an at-home, in-bed, soup-drinking kind of guy. We're going to close this case, and he's unlikely to compromise on that front.

CHAPTER 23

THE SHERIFF'S STATION is unusually quiet. Deputy Baird, a.k.a. Furious Monkeys, is the only visible employee.

She briefly glances up as I enter, so I approach the desk and risk a question. "Hey, did they finally release the new levels in that game?"

Shockingly, she pauses her app and smiles broadly. "I just hit level 450. And I was the first one this time. So if that hotshot photographer, Superbomb, is in town, be sure to rub it in for me."

I barely understand the gamer rivalry, but I remember how shocked she was to learn Quince Knudsen was basically a Furious Monkeys rock star. "Oh, I will definitely let him know. Is Sheriff Harper in his office?"

"I think he already headed into the interrogation room. He said you should join him as soon as you got here."

"All right. Thanks. Good luck keeping one step ahead of Quince."

Her expression turns deadly serious, and she nods once before returning to her game.

Knocking lightly on the door, I hear Erick's response within. "Come in."

Easing the door open, I smile and nod. "Hi, Kurt. I hope it's all right with you if I sit in."

He avoids making eye contact but tips his head toward the empty seat. "Sure. Sheriff Harper said you might have some helpful information."

That statement would indicate that Erick has kept his cards close to the vest so far. For once, I'll follow his lead instead of taking over and pushing things in my own direction. Grabbing the available chair next to Erick, I slide it back and sit casually across from Kurt. He has some water to his left, and his fingers nervously rub the paper cup.

Erick makes a show of removing his pad and paper, flipping to a blank page, and clearing his throat. "Kurt, I believe you made a false confession. I'd like to give you the opportunity to correct your statement. Would you like to do that?"

At first, Kurt stubbornly plans to stick to the story. He shakes his head and twists the paper cup against the table.

Erick unrolls the next bit of information. "During the course of our investigation, we discovered your father, Marcus Frazier, was killed in an arson fire in Québec City. I've ordered copies of the complete report and the postmortem. You are welcome to take a look at those if you choose to. Is there anything you'd like to tell me?"

Waves of shock and resignation fill the room. It's clear Kurt wasn't sure, but on some level, he suspected his father was dead.

"Kurt. We've apprehended the man responsible. He's confessed to setting the arena fire."

At this statement, Kurt's gaze finally lifts from the cup of liquid to meet Erick's. A strange peacefulness washes over him. "Is that true? You're not just making it up to try to get me to say something?"

Sheriff Harper slowly places his pen across the notepad and gazes directly into Kurt's eyes. "I don't believe in manipulation or playing games. Your father died in an arson-set fire nearly five years ago. The arsonist, a Mr. Gammon, is responsible for five other fires in Canada, and he's confessed to setting the arena fire here in Pin Cherry Harbor. All the fires were set with his signature method. Now, I'll ask you again, do you wish to amend your statement?"

Kurt drops his head into his hands, and silent sobs shake his shoulders. "At first, I thought he did it. I thought Dad turned his back on us and set fire to the arena to punish me for— For putting the trophy where he could never get his hands on it."

A tendril of icy chill circles my left ring finger. While Erick continues talking to Kurt, I glance down at my ring.

The golden curling trophy appears to be stuffed in a dark cubby, covered with dust. It's hardly an image that supports the treasure lounging at the bottom of the great lake.

Without thinking, I blurt, "Where's the trophy, Kurt?"

Erick's head spins, as though on a lazy-Susan, and his expression is a mix of irritation and concern.

I might've interrupted something important, but I wasn't paying attention to what was going on in the room. I was busy in my special otherworld, where useful information makes itself known at some of the most inconvenient times.

Kurt's entire demeanor changes. He angles back in the chair, crosses his arms, and once again gazes toward the floor.

Erick arches an eyebrow in my general direction, and I nod toward my ring. He picks up his pen and taps it on the pad. "Kurt, what year did you steal the trophy?"

"I don't remember exactly. Maybe, like, four or four and a half years ago."

"Did you steal the trophy as ransom for your father?"

Kurt falls deadly silent and still.

Erick leans forward and lowers his voice to that grumbly, growly level that means business. "Kurt. The curling club is willing to drop all charges and reinstate you at the new arena. But you've gotta come clean with me right now."

The accused's eyes ping-pong from Erick to me and back to Erick. "New arena? What are you talking about?"

And that's my cue. "My father and I are ready to rebuild the entire facility. Hockey rinks, curling sheets, figure skating arenas . . . Everything. We're even planning to build a replica trophy."

At the mention of a new trophy, Kurt fidgets in his seat and looks away.

Exhaling softly, I lighten my tone. "Unless, of course, the original trophy didn't end up at the bottom of the lake. Maybe it's tucked in a nice little dusty corner somewhere. Maybe it was supposed to be your get-out-of-jail-free card with whoever was harassing your father. But if that was the case, why didn't you give it to them or to Rory Bombay?"

At the mention of the dark sorcerer, Kurt shakes uncontrollably. "What about him? Is he in custody?"

Placing a hand on Sheriff Harper's arm, I field

the question. "Unfortunately, he was killed during a hostage rescue. He refused to surrender and planned to leave the country with an unwilling human shield."

Kurt Frazier's entire body seems to turn to jelly. Every bit of tension that locked his muscles in place evaporates. "Are you sure he's really dead?"

Erick's jaw flexes once. "Frank Freeman, a.k.a. Rory Bombay, is definitely deceased. The post-mortem will be available tomorrow."

My suspicions about what had been terrifying Kurt are finally confirmed.

Kurt Frazier's resolve, or maybe it was loyalty, finally crumbles. "Okay, Sheriff, I didn't set the fire at the arena. That Bombay guy told me I had to steal the trophy in exchange for my dad's life. Then he said he had a guy who would make it all look like a big accident, and no one would ever know the trophy was missing. I never expected him to kill me as part of the cover-up."

Erick jots a few notes in his notepad. "Kurt, I'm going to turn on the recording device, and I'll ask you to repeat that for the record. Officially."

Kurt does as he's asked and continues. "I didn't want to tell Bombay the trophy in the arena was a fake. I was worried about my dad, you know? I didn't know my pop was already dead." He clears his throat and leans toward us. "Last time, the ransom texts just stopped. I figured it had been my dad trying another angle— And he got picked up for something else before he could arrange a drop."

"Why didn't you return the trophy?" I'm seriously confused by Kurt's logic.

He shrugs. "Why should I? They didn't deserve it. I'd already swapped it out for a fake . . ."

Erick taps his pen. "Of course. I'd be surprised if the fake would have fooled a collector like Bombay. Did you steal the substitute trophy?"

"Yeah. Yeah, I stole it, and I left it in a dumpster. Just following the instructions from Bombay."

"Understood. Did you hang around to see if he picked it up?"

"No way. That guy gave me the creeps. When he was around, I felt like I didn't quite have control of myself. I dropped the trophy and made a run for it."

The sheriff leans back, runs his left thumb along his jawline, and nods. "And what was the arrangement to collect your father? Were you supposed to pick him up somewhere?"

The look on Kurt's face is one of hurt and shock. "I don't know. At the time, it all seemed so clear, but now I don't ever remember talking about that part."

I glance at Erick and inhale sharply. Knowing what he now knows about Rory Bombay, I'm sure a smart cookie like Sheriff Harper can imagine the kind of mental manipulations that were used to deceive Kurt.

Erick picks up his pen, moves to make a note, but instead places the pen back on the table. "And what about the fire? Did you ever see who started it? Or knocked you out?"

"No. Honest, Sheriff. I was working my regular shift, and I thought I heard something fall in the supply closet. It's not unheard of. Sometimes things get put away in a hurry—you know."

Sheriff Harper nods.

"So I went in to see if I needed to straighten up, and the next thing I know, something cracks me on the back of the skull, and down I go."

"It was my understanding you were on the phone with your mother at the time. Is that true?"

Kurt takes a long drink of water and glances up to the left. Theoretically, accessing an actual memory. "Yeah. Yeah, that's right. I was letting her know I wasn't going to make it over for supper. I try to have supper with her a couple times a week. Then I think that's when I got cracked on the skull. It's all a little fuzzy, Sheriff."

"Understood. How's your head feeling now?"

Kurt reaches back and runs his fingers along the lump on his skull. "It's pretty tender. But the swelling has gone down."

Erick makes a note on his pad and glances at me from the corner of his eye.

If this is a bit more of our nonverbal communication at work, I hope I'm interpreting it properly and taking my cue. "Kurt, I really need you to tell me where that trophy is."

He exhales and collapses onto the table. His left hand knocks the cup to the floor, but fortunately, it's empty.

"Look, no one's trying to pin any charges on you. I can't speak for Sheriff Harper, but if the trophy is recovered unharmed, I think we can wrap it all up in this arson incident. No one has to know about what happened years ago."

Erick raises an eyebrow and shrugs. "You have my word, Kurt. You lead us to that trophy, and I will log it into evidence as part of the ongoing investigation. I'll keep your name out of it."

The beleaguered man leans back, and a couple of tears trickle down his cheek. "Toss me in the back of the cruiser, Sheriff. I'll take you there now."

I'm so excited that the vision in my ring is actually leading somewhere; I want to leap up on the table and dance an Irish jig. However, I've learned a great deal about decorum since my arrival in Pin Cherry Harbor. I casually rise from my chair and hold the door open for Sheriff Too-Hot-To-Handle and Kurt Frazier.

Our guide gives Erick directions to his apartment near the Birch County Community College. I inwardly chuckle as I think about my undercover archaeology case at that facility, but that's another story.

We park, and Kurt leads us up to his second-floor apartment.

Once inside, he takes us to the closet in his bedroom. He slides the hangers to the left and loosens the screws on a grate near the floor.

Two things you should know: No contractor in their right mind puts a heating vent in a closet. That should be anyone's first clue. And the second thing is the size of the grate. It's three times as high as any normal heating register. Once Kurt removes the finger-tight screws, he reaches inside and pulls out a dusty pillowcase. As the fabric falls away, the trophy reveals itself. It may have lost a bit of its original shine, but a solid gold replica curling stone is impressive, regardless.

Erick accepts the trophy from Kurt and smiles. "This feels like the real thing. Let me give Paulsen a quick call. She's organizing Gammon's extradition to Canada, and I'm sure CC would like to be the one to present this to the Curling Federation."

Kurt gets to his feet and brushes the dust from his knees.

I grip Erick's arm and hold up one finger. "If we

can hold off on that for maybe just an hour or two. I'd like to rally the troops over at the arena and get those photos. I guarantee it will get picked up nationally, maybe even internationally, if we have that trophy in the photo, Sheriff."

Erick grins and shakes his head. "Maybe you missed your calling, Moon. You obviously make a great heiress, but it seems like you'd make a heck of a media maven as well."

We say our goodbyes to Kurt. He promises to stay out of trouble and looks forward to rejoining the team out at the new arena.

CHAPTER 24

Erick drives while I make arrangements.

"Hey, Dad, you know that whole arena-building thing we talked about?" He chuckles his confirmation. "Can you meet me over at the arena in about thirty minutes? I'll get Quince over there and we'll get that photo shoot knocked out. Wear something that makes you look like a super important businessman." I can barely hear his reply through the laughter, but I think it's safe to assume he'll be there.

Next call: Quince Knudsen. "Hey, Quince. I know you said 2:30, but things got a little wadded up on my end. Can you meet us there in about thirty?"

His only reply is, "Lit. Magic hour."

Luckily, my somewhat extensive background in

film and television translates that reply. The magic hour is that beautiful sixty-ish minutes between the sun slipping toward the horizon and the sun slipping below the horizon. It's not a time to take photos of the sunset per se, but rather turn the camera in the opposite direction and snap images of the way the beautiful golds and pinks play off the landscape.

"See you there, Quince."

Erick points a thumb toward my T-shirt and shrugs. "I heard you tell your dad to dress professionally. Should I stop by your apartment so you can do the same?"

We share a giggle, but the man knows what he's talking about.

He waits in the cruiser, keeping an eye on the trophy, while I run upstairs and insist on Grams picking the quickest outfit in history!

"Oh, Mitzy! You certainly know how to take the fun out of everything."

"Well, if your definition of fun is posing in front of the burned-out shell of a once-bustling ice arena, then, yes, I suppose I do."

"Point taken." She flits around the closet like a hummingbird that's overdosed on nectar. "You mentioned something about magic hour. So we want to avoid anything that would fall in that color range. I think your black skinny jeans and those lovely leather riding boots are the perfect start. Now, we need a sweater that whispers hometown hero without being too narcissistic."

I flop onto the bed and sigh in exasperation. Dear Lord, baby Jesus. I've never heard anyone anthropomorphize clothing the way this woman can.

"I know I'm not supposed to listen, but I heard that! Now stop wasting your time sulking and get in the bathroom and do something with your haystack of a hairdo. And put on some makeup. The flash will wash you out. We don't need folks thinking an actual ghost is responsible for rebuilding the arena!"

She laughs herself near senseless with that hilarious quip.

Twenty minutes later, I'm dressed, coiffed, and have practiced what Grams considers an appropriate smile.

As I head downstairs to rejoin Erick in the cruiser, I run my hand over the magenta cowl-neck sweater. It does set off my hair nicely, and I'm sure it will look great against the snowy and yet charred background.

When I reach the cruiser, I'm shocked to see someone in the backseat. Opening the passenger door, I look in and gasp. "Dad? Did you climb in there of your own free will?"

He and Erick both share a laugh at my expense.

"Yes, sweetie. It wasn't my first choice to ride in

the back of a police cruiser, but I thought I'd spare you the indignity. Erick will stick with us for the photo shoot and serve as security for the trophy. Looks like Isadora picked the perfect outfit."

I glance at his light-blue button-down shirt and upscale tweed jacket. "Looks like Amaryllis didn't do so bad on your outfit either."

He blushes and shrugs his shoulders. "Hey, everyone has to play to their strengths, right?"

"Can confirm."

As I close my door, Erick backs out of the alley and heads toward the arena. When we arrive, Quince is already on site, walking the perimeter in search of the perfect shot.

I have to say, the Duncan-Moon Foundation setting up a photojournalism scholarship at the local high school that sent Quince Knudsen directly to Columbia was one of the best ideas I've ever had.

"Hey, I'm supposed to tell you that you got powned—or is it poned? Anyway, Baird got to 450 before you."

The capable photographer chuckles. "Gunand-Badge crushed."

My message of gameworld dominance has been delivered. Time to get posing.

Since young, yet old-fashioned, Quince insists on using a 35mm film camera, there aren't any proofs for my father and I to check. However, I trust the boy genius implicitly, and I can't wait for the good news to hit the town in tomorrow's paper.

Quince foregoes any verbose exit and simply nods and hops into his janky beat-up truck.

Erick drops my father and me off at the alley between our properties and insists on getting the trophy straight back to the station so it can be prepped for transport to Canada.

He bwaaps the siren once as he pulls away, just to mess with me.

"Thanks for going through all that rigmarole with me, Dad."

He bends and scoops an arm around my shoulders. "Anything for you, Princess."

"Dad! We've been over this! I'm a grown woman. And I have a name."

He takes a step back and bows clumsily. "Begging your pardon, Mizithra."

Blerg. "Will I see you and Amaryllis at the Yuletide Extravaganza?"

His grey eyes sparkle. "You betcha. We wouldn't miss it for the world."

Weird. "All right. Grams has a whole thing planned, so I better get in there and get crackin', or I'll never be ready by the time Erick finishes his paperwork and swings by to pick me up."

"Sounds good, honey. See you later."

Upstairs, Ghost-ma has prepped the bathroom

vanity as though she's been hired as the makeup artist on a big-budget motion picture. I don't know where in the world all the makeup came from, but I'm growing concerned about her and Pyewacket and their "learning to online shop."

"I hope you're not planning on putting all of that on my face, Grams. I need to be able to make actual expressions."

"Don't you fret, sweetie. I'm an absolute expert at making hours of effort appear effortless."

"Fantastic. Hair and makeup first, then clothes?"

"Oh, sweetie. Your naïveté is adorable. The sweater will have to go on first because it slips over the hair and face. Then we'll protect the collar with some clean paper towels. And once we've completed hair and makeup, you can slip into the rest of your outfit. And don't forget, that glorious faux fur coat is your *pièce de résistance*."

"Don't worry, Grams. If I forget, I'm sure you'll remind me."

She whoops with laughter as she slips into the bathroom to plug in the styling wand.

Hours later, or, honestly, it could be days, she pronounces me perfect.

I turn back and forth in front of the mirror and barely recognize the reflection. "You have a magic touch, Isadora. There's no way in the world I could've gotten this airbrushed, magazine-cover-ready, viral-selfie look all by myself."

"Ree-ow." Soft but condescending.

"Hey, no smart-aleck remarks from the peanut gallery, fuzzball."

"Ree-OW!" A warning punctuated by a threat.

"I'm kidding. I'm kidding. Consider the phrase stricken from my vocabulary. I love you completely, and I live only to serve you, Your Majesty."

"Re-ow." Forgiven.

BING. BONG. BING.

Grams and I, as usual, cry out in unison, "He's here!"

I slip into the pale-blue cloud of a coat, carefully adjust the earmuffs until they meet with Ghost-ma's approval, and grab the white suede mittens.

By the time I reach the bottom of the wrought-iron circular staircase, I'm sweating. Sure, it's a little uncomfortable right now, but once I step into the polar outdoors, I'm sure I'll be pleased.

When I open the door, Erick exhales deeply and nods his approval. "You look good enough to eat."

"I hope that means I look beautiful and not that I look as big as a giant cake!"

He smirks. "Let me flip a coin."

"Rude."

"I'm only kidding, Moon. You look gorgeous. I feel like a pathetic slob next to your royal beauty."

His comment causes me to scan him from head to toe. He's wearing a very fashionable pair of charcoal-grey woolen pants, a snug cable-knit sweater that emphasizes all of his lovely assets, and a handsome parka. His normally slicked-back hair is totally free of pomade and tousled in a devil-may-care yummy way all around his handsome face.

"You don't look so bad yourself, Sheriff."

Erick offers me his arm. "Allow me to escort you to your chariot, milady."

Glancing up and down the alley, I see no means of conveyance. And I grow more alarmed by the moment. He's not leading me toward the street; he's leading me toward the frozen lake.

If I spent two hours getting ready only to rip across the snow on the back of a snowmobile, I'm going to be mildly miffed.

As we round the corner, I hear the whine and yip of dogs. Along the edge of the frozen great lake sit eight sled dogs harnessed to a genuine Inuit snow sled. Manning the controls is a form I'd recognize anywhere.

"Silas? How did you get roped into this?"

Erick responds. "I was going to take you to the extravaganza on my own, but after I got shot—"

Silas pipes up. "Ever since I competed in the

Beargrease marathon, I've been eager to get behind another team. I practically begged the sheriff to allow me this fantastic opportunity."

Wow, this day could not get any weirder. "All right. Somebody better show me how to hang onto this thing."

Erick folds back the layers of hides and takes the first seat. He helps me into his lap, wedged between his strong legs, and pulls the furs up around us. I feel quite cozy and slightly titillated.

Silas shouts a command. "Hup. Hup. Hup."

The team of dogs launches into action as though their very lives depend on it. As we glide under the starry sky, the moonlight sparkles off the snow and seems to turn the drifts into mountains of diamonds.

Silas shouts a new command. "Ha." The dogs arc to the left.

As we near the town square, which abuts the lake, the flickering glow of the enormous ice castle takes my breath away.

Erick hugs his arms around me and kisses my neck. "What do you think?"

"Oh, my gosh! It's so gorgeous."

A call of "Gee" comes from the driver, and the sled team eases to the right.

I feel dragging from the rear of the sled, as Silas

must be using whatever it is they use for a brake on one of these things.

We pull up next to the castle, and instead of marching straight to the mulled-cider tent, Erick takes me into the castle through a secret back entrance. I definitely don't remember seeing this in previous years.

When we reach the main room of the ice castle, a harpist begins to play "Hungry Like the Wolf."

All of my psychic senses tingle, but the only message I can get is that gosh darn image of a snow princess.

Erick takes my hands and turns me a quarter turn, for some reason, then kisses me softly.

The excitement and anticipation rolling off him nearly knock me over. Luckily, he has a tight grip on my hands.

"Mitzy, I knew the moment you tripped and fell on me that you were the gal for me." He grins nervously.

I open my mouth to protest, but I swear there's a hum of chuckles floating on the breeze.

He squeezes my hands and continues. "Every day I get to spend with you is better than the one before. Thank you for choosing to make Pin Cherry Harbor your home."

Tears are building in the corners of my eyes, but the distant sound of mumbled cheers keeps the waterworks at bay. Glancing around the sparkly ice palace, I confirm we are alone.

Erick swallows audibly and takes a deep, shaky breath.

Then . . . it happens.

He drops to one knee, reaches into the pocket of his parka, and opens a small golden box.

"Mitzy Moon, you're the most infuriatingly amazing woman I've ever met. And I'd like you to keep challenging me until the day I die. Will you marry me?"

Gazing down at the ring, I instantly recognize the precious heirloom I rescued from the lining of my grandmother's vintage coat. A plain circle of gold, with barely a flake of a diamond in the setting. This is the very ring Odell gave Isadora when he proposed to her. Or, as she was known then, Myrtle.

Erick remains on one knee and waves his hand nervously. "Hey, Moon, are you gonna answer?"

Falling to my knees beside him, I throw my arms around his neck and kiss him foolishly. "Of course, I'll marry you! I can't imagine spending my life with anyone else. And I'm happy to keep challenging you as long as you promise to keep bringing out the best in me."

He kisses me as though we've never kissed before. And the image of this absolutely magical moment will literally never fade from my mind.

Is it my imagination, or do I hear applause?

Erick blushes and pulls another item from his coat.

A tiara!

"Not on your life, Harper."

He casually points to something clamped to a block of ice to the left of us, which looks suspiciously like a camera, and leans in to whisper, "Your grandmother insisted it would be necessary to complete the Snow Princess ruse." He grins sheepishly.

I lower my head in defeat, knowing Grams and Pye are watching over a Phoom connection, and he removes my earmuffs and fits the tiara in place.

As we emerge from the ice castle, the square is brimming over with familiar faces, most of them are gazing up at a jumbotron and cheering along with a running loop of the proposal.

Howie "How to" Fairlane waves from the crowd, confirming my hi-tech suspicions, and I surreptitiously punch Erick in the gut. "So much for the town that tech forgot, Sheriff."

The mayor steps up, microphone in hand, and adds to my mortification. He slips a sparkly blue-and-white sash over my head and announces, "Ladies and gentlemen, let's hear it for our first annual Northern Lights Yuletide Extravaganza Snow Princess!"

The crowd goes wild, and Erick joins the raucous applause.

An unofficial receiving line forms.

First in line is the indomitable Gracie Harper. She throws her arms around me and woots. "Welcome to the family, sweetheart. I'm sorry it took my stubborn son so long to recognize the truth."

Beside me, Erick groans. "Mom, come on. You promised to behave."

She giggles. "When have I ever behaved?" Gracie grabs the hand of a woman who could be her twin and pulls the shy gal forward. "Mitzy, this is my baby sister, Hope. Hope, meet the woman who put my Ricky on the path to happiness."

Yeesh! Gracie is putting an awful lot of responsibility on my shoulders. Apparently, she has no idea what her heroic son has done to tame my wild side and save my backside!

Hope steps forward and fumbles a handshake into an awkward hug. "Nice to meet you, Miss Moon."

She may look like her sister, but she is the emotional polar opposite. Definite introvert. I lower my voice and speak soothingly. "It's so nice to meet you, Hope. Please let Erick and me know if there is anything—absolutely anything—that you and Gracie ever need. Oh, and we're happy to fly you both up to visit anytime."

Hope gently touches my arm and leans in. "Would it be okay to send Gracie up on her own sometimes?"

The unspoken need to have a break from her new permanent houseguest doesn't miss my radar. "You betcha!" I wink and smile.

She exhales with relief, and the line of well-wishers surges forward.

Each hand I shake warms my heart a little more. Doc Ledo, pushed by Tilly, followed by Tally and Tatum. Next comes Lars and a few of the regulars from Final Destination.

Quince and the elder Knudsen approach, and I brace myself for a lecture on the history of ice—or worse.

Thankfully, Quince finds his voice first. "My dad bumped the arena story below the fold. He said nothing could beat this for the top story."

"Please tell me you got my good side."

The young photographer blushes. "They're all good, dude."

A familiar cackle resounds through the throng as Twiggy and Wayne approach.

"Hey, I thought you guys were in Fiji?"

Twiggy smirks. "I wouldn't have missed this show for all the kava in the world, kid. 'Bout damn time, Sheriff." She playfully punches him on the arm—the good one, luckily.

Jacob, Amaryllis, Stellen, and even the spritely Yolo pass by and offer their congratulations. There's a serious moment between Jacob and Erick, but eventually, my dad cracks a smile, and they exchange a bro hug.

Nimkii hugs me and offers to cater the wedding, while Anne promises to bake the wedding cake of the century.

"Thanks, guys. I haven't gotten that far down the road, but those are both wonderful offers."

As Artie approaches, an uncharacteristic tear trickles from her eye. "I won't forget what you did for my boy, Mitzy. You better believe your street will be the first one plowed from now on—right after the hospital."

As if on cue, thick white flakes flutter from the sparkling sky. It feels like twinkles of stardust are blessing our day.

Last, but never least, Silas and Odell bring up the rear.

Odell claps Erick on the arm and chokes back emotion. "That ring holds a lifetime of love. I hope it brings you both everything you deserve."

Erick silently nods his thanks, and Odell kisses me on the cheek. "You're one in a million, kid."

"You too, Gramps."

The crowd disperses, and Silas offers to buy us mulled ciders.

However, before we make it two strides toward the fabled tent, Lars grabs the abandoned mic from the stand.

"Fifty-cent beers for the next hour at Final Destination! And we'll set up the karaoke machine, folks. When you finish your ciders, head over for a song or two." He turns to Erick and me. "Consider it your engagement party, Daisy!"

His reference to my undercover barmaid gig brings uproarious laughter from too many folks.

Erick takes my hand and shrugs. "Karaoke?"

Tilting my head upward, I grin smugly. "Born to."

CHAPTER 25

BEFORE ENTERTAINING ANY KARAOKE NONSENSE, I insist we follow Silas to the glögg tent. As the spiced liquid warms my tummy, Erick's loving gaze warms my heart.

Silas awkwardly clears his throat. "If you'll be needing an officiant, I am certainly able to make myself available."

I clink my mug against his, wink, and whisper, "I guess that will be up to Grams, Mr. Willoughby."

The three of us chuckle in the perfectly crisp night air.

As we move away from the beverage tent, cupping our hands around the delicious steaming cider, an impromptu procession forms behind us. Friends, family, and the curious, fall in line as we make our way toward Final Destination.

Poor Erick. I'm an old hand at karaoke. I've screeched out the classics from atop the stage, a stool, and even a bar more times than I care to remember. Thankfully, my kind-hearted boyfriend is going along for the ride without protest.

Our parade wends its way through the booths in the town square and down the road. It's not far, and the brisk pace keeps the blood pumping.

The flickering neon sign grows closer.

Inside the dive bar, tattered holiday decorations hang haphazardly from beer logo signs and long-broken singing fish on plaques.

Lars has some help behind the bar, and I head over to get the details.

"Hey, Tatum. Are you working two jobs now?"

She grins, and her eyes search the crowd for Quince. "We're talking about getting a place together next year. Just trying to make extra money as fast as I can." Her cheeks flush.

Reaching across the bar, I squeeze her hand and grin broadly. "Awesome. You know I was pulling for you guys straight from the beginning, right?"

She giggles and looks away. "You're the best. My mom always says it, but I'm totally on board." Tatum swallows and bites her bottom lip.

"What is it? You can say anything to me. Trust me, I've heard it all."

Tatum leans forward and lowers her voice. "That proposal was epic."

It's my turn to blush. "It was pretty flippin' romantic. Although, I could've done without the big screen replay." I jerk my thumb over my shoulder toward Erick as he chats up Wayne and Twiggy. "He always keeps me guessing. I suppose that's a good thing."

Tatum nods. "I think you're right."

Lars steps onto the tiny stage and for the second time this evening, commandeers a microphone. "Hey, clear off that middle table for the bride-and-groom-to-be. Hank is taking your karaoke requests on the slips of paper. And print clearly. Hank can see about as good as a catfish in a shallow crick."

I certainly don't get the analogy, but make a mental note to print clearly if I choose to sing.

A dilapidated three-ring binder is making the rounds, and Twiggy takes the stage to get things started. She sings a series of familiar Christmas carols to buy time while other future performers make their song selections. She ends with a moving rendition of "Silent Night," and no one makes a sound. Ironic? Not sure.

Hank calls out the next singer, and the game is afoot. Some songs match their performers to a "T," but others are truly shocking. For instance, when the petite fairy-like creature Yolo takes the stage and belts out a near-flawless rendition of Sia's "Chandelier," the crowd rockets to their feet for a standing ovation.

Twiggy wickedly writes in a selection for me, and the next thing I know, I'm on stage doing my best with an off-key version of "These Boots Are Made for Walkin'" by Nancy Sinatra.

Fortunately, the crowd sings along for support, and it's a forgiving environment. Maybe it's the mulled cider or the spiced rum shot someone bought me, but I feel like I did a decent job.

Jacob gives us an also passable performance of "Mack the Knife."

My tummy is warm and tingly, and happiness virtually oozes from my pores. I'm feeling pretty good about myself when Hank calls out the next singer on the roster. "Sheriff Harper. You're up."

Erick lifts a hand to wave off the request and shakes his head.

Deputies Johnson and Gilbert, drinking soda water and pretending to be security, laugh and punch each other from their post next to the front door. Seems like a serious dereliction of duty, but I suppose they have their radios, and the noticeably absent Deputy Paulsen would be sure to call them to respond to the slightest infraction.

Erick spies them across the dimly lit bar and

wags his finger in warning. The two deputies attempt to straighten up and stifle their laughter.

Hank raises a hand to shade his eyes from the single spotlight and calls out again. "You know the rules, Sheriff Harper. I call your name. You get on the stage."

Wow. They take their karaoke very seriously at this latitude.

A few people in the crowd clap, and others chant, "Sher-iff. Sher-iff. Sher-iff."

At long last, Erick succumbs to the pressure and heads toward the stage. He blinks in the bright spotlight, looks left and right to locate the screen scrolling the lyrics, and gives Hank a finger gun.

The opening bars of the song are unmistakable. I must've watched *Willy Wonka and the Chocolate Factory* at least a hundred times as a child. There's no missing the opening of "The Candy Man."

When Erick begins the song, I look around to see if someone is playing a practical joke. He has the voice of an angel, and Sammy Davis Jr. himself couldn't sing it any better. Maybe Hank left the vocal track on just to help the sheriff out. Nope, Erick adlibs a couple doo wops in between the next stanza, and I'm frozen in awe.

Yet another thing I didn't know about my now fiancé! Erick Harper is crooning like an old-school movie star.

He continues to belt out the stanzas, and several members of the audience wave a lighter or their phone's flashlight app as they all get behind his gorgeous performance.

I'm losing track of all the things the man can do when he steps off the tiny stage, shaking hands here and there. Wait—

A ripple of fear crawls across my shoulders. He's coming for me. He's going to sing to me.

Like a deer trapped in the headlights, I want to run away but can't move.

Erick approaches the table during the musical bridge, extends a hand toward me, and curls his finger in a come-hither gesture.

Shaking my head, I wave it away, hoping that's the end of it.

Over the swelling music, he speaks into the microphone. "Hey, folks, can we give my fiancée a little encouragement?"

Raucous cheers of "Mitzy! Mitzy! Mitzy!" resound through the small establishment.

If I don't get up and give in, things will only get worse. I place my hand in his, swallow what is left of my pride, and follow him to the stage.

He pulls me up next to him and sings the final refrain straight into my beet-red face. My lips may be pressed tightly together, but I hope he's receiving the daggers shooting from my eyes.

The song ends. He grips me, dips me, and kisses me passionately in front of half the town! The emotion in his kiss erases the rest of the world, and I barely hear the microphone bounce to the floor.

However, the unmistakable cackle floating up from the audience cannot be ignored. Twiggy shouts from the back. "Nice mic drop, Sheriff!"

Laughter ripples through the room as Erick returns me to my feet, grabs my hand, and bows to the audience—Broadway-musical style.

Just when I thought I had it all figured out . . .

End of Book 21

But, the mysteries continue...
Curl up with the next book in the spinoff Harper and Moon Investigations series!

A NOTE FROM TRIXIE

They're engaged! I hope you're ready to join Mitzy and Erick on their new adventures in *Harper and Moon Investigations*—headed your way in Spring 2023. As always, I'll keep writing them if you keep reading . . .

The best part of "living" in Pin Cherry Harbor continues to be feedback from my early readers. Thank you to my alpha readers/cheerleaders, Angel and Michael. HUGE thanks to my fantastic beta readers who continue to give me extremely useful and honest feedback: Veronica McIntyre and Nadine Peterse-Vrijhof. And big "small town" hugs to the world's best ARC Team – Trixie's Mystery ARC Detectives!

My diligent editor Philip Newey definitely helped me plug some gaping plot holes. Many thanks to him! I enjoy getting notes and polishing each story. I'd also like to give buckets of gratitude to Roxx at Proof Perfect for the stellar proofing! Any remaining errors are my own.

Here's to hoping you have a holiday as joyous as Mitzy's!

FUN FACT: I learned the dogsled lingo from an actual Iditarod musher, and stood on the back of the very sled I described in the story.

My favorite line from this case: "If I spent two hours getting ready only to rip across the snow on the back of a snowmobile, I'm going to be mildly miffed." ~Mitzy

I'm currently writing book one in the *Harper and Moon Investigations* series. All your *Mitzy Moon Mysteries* series favorites will continue on—but there will be a few "shake ups" in town.

I hope you'll continue to hang out with us.

Trixie Silvertale (November 2022)

Harper and Moon Investigations No. 1

A pattern of murder. A threadbare case. Can our psychic sleuth pick out the guilty before time spools out?

Mitzy Moon is finally tying the knot. And she's loving the whole town's excitement for their upcoming big day. But when their tailor is found buttons up behind a jazz lounge, the almost-newlyweds will have to hem in a murderer before their dreams rip apart at the seams.

Knowing they'll get no help from the new sheriff in town, the couple embarks on a tightly woven undercover assignment. But Mitzy fails to heed ominous warnings from her mentor, Ghost-ma, and her entitled feline. When another body drops, she could be the next target erased by the mounting powers in the darkness...

Can Mitzy and Erick unravel the twisted clues, or will their wedding be eclipsed by a funeral?

Bells and Bombshells is the first book in a hilarious new paranormal cozy mystery series, Harper and Moon Investigations. If you like snarky heroines, supernatural intrigue, and a dash of romance, then you'll love Trixie Silvertale's wedded whodunit.

Buy *Bells and Bombshells* to stitch up a killer today!

Grab yours!
https://readerlinks.com/l/5211927

Scan this QR Code with the camera on your phone. You'll be taken right to the next Harper and Moon Investigations case!

SPECIAL INVITATION . . .

Come visit Pin Cherry Harbor!

Get access to the Exclusive Mitzy Moon Mysteries character quiz – free!

Find out which character you are in Pin Cherry Harbor and see if you have what it takes to be part of Mitzy's gang.

This quiz is only available to members of the Paranormal Cozy Club, Trixie Silvertale's reader group.

Visit the link below to join the club and get access to the quiz:

Join Trixie's Club
https://trixiesilvertale.com/paranormal-cozy-club/

Once you're in the Club, you'll also be the first to receive updates from Pin Cherry Harbor and access to giveaways, new release announcements, short stories, behind-the-scenes secrets, and much more!

Scan this QR Code with the camera on your phone. You'll be taken right to the page to join the Club!

THANK YOU!

Trying out a new book is always a risk and I'm thankful that you rolled the dice with Mitzy Moon. If you loved the book, the sweetest thing you can do (*even sweeter than pin cherry pie à la mode*) is to leave a review so that other readers will take a chance on Mitzy and the gang.

Don't feel you have to write a book report. A brief comment like, "Can't wait to read the next book in this series!" will help potential readers make their choice.

★★★★★

Leave a quick review HERE
https://readerlinks.com/l/2985040

★★★★★

Thank you kindly, and I'll see you in Pin Cherry Harbor!

Chocolate Crinkle Cookie Murder

...more to come!

MAGICAL RENAISSANCE FAIRE MYSTERIES

Explore the world of Coriander the Conjurer. A fortune-telling fairy with a heart of gold!

Book 1:

All Swell That Ends Spell – A dubious festival. A fatal swim. Can this fortune-telling fairy herald the true killer?

Book 2:

Fairy Wives of Windsor – A jolly Faire. A shocking murder. Can this furtive fairy outsmart the killer?

Book 3:

Double Double Royal Trouble – When a treat-peddling witch is found dead, will this cursed faire crumble?

Join Sydney Coleman and her unruly ghosts, as they solve mysteries in a truly haunted mansion!

Book 1: **Moonlight and Mischief** – She's desperate for a fresh start, but is a mansion on sale too good to be true?

Book 2: **Moonlight and Magic** – A haunted Halloween tour seem like the perfect plan, until there's murder...

Book 3: ***Moonlight and Mayhem*** – An unwelcome visitor. A surprising past. Will her fire sale end in smoke?

ABOUT THE AUTHOR

USA TODAY Bestselling author Trixie Silvertale grew up reading an endless supply of Lilian Jackson Braun, Hardy Boys, and Nancy Drew novels. She loves the amateur sleuths in cozy mysteries and obsesses about all things paranormal. Those two passions unite in all her cozy mysteries, and she's thrilled to write them and share them with you.

When she's not consumed by writing, she bakes to fuel her creative engine and pulls weeds in her herb garden to clear her head (*and sometimes she pulls out her hair, but mostly weeds*).

Greetings are welcome:
trixie@trixiesilvertale.com

f facebook.com/TrixieSilvertale

⊙ instagram.com/trixiesilvertale

BB bookbub.com/authors/trixie-silvertale